BABY BY CHRISTMAS

THE MCINTYRE MEN
BOOK FIVE

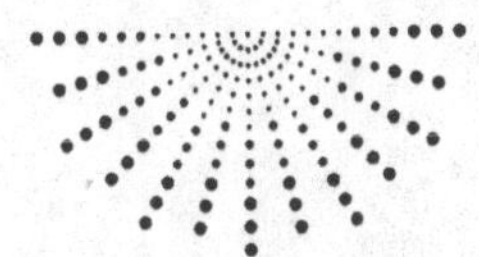

MAGGIE SHAYNE
JESSICA LEWIS

OLIVERHEBERBOOKS

CHAPTER ONE

MARCH 29TH

Alexis Wakeland had never started a bar fight before. It would probably surprise her family to hear that. She'd always been the black sheep, the one the others rolled their eyes at when they thought she wasn't looking. She was the hellion who got into more trouble than the rest of her siblings put together, the one who made bad choices and couldn't admit she was wrong. Despite all that, she'd never once been the cause of a barroom brawl--until tonight.

All she'd wanted was a fun night out with her big brother. A couple of drinks and laughs before he deployed to Afghanistan. You couldn't blame her for being sentimental. She was afraid she'd never see him again.

Like Jeff. Angie's husband had died over there. And now Allie's big sister was a widow, raising two kids alone.

Poor little Jack still refused to believe his daddy was really gone.

Allie would never *ever* be a military wife. It couldn't possibly be worth that kind of pain. Some days she couldn't imagine how her big sister managed to get out of bed every morning, and face every day without Jeff. The two had always been like clouds and sky, inseparable. One couldn't exist without the other.

Yet somehow, her sister kept going.

And their brother Adam was deploying tomorrow.

Adam was also talking to her, but she wasn't listening. "I love you, you know," she blurted.

He was quiet for a second. Then he said, "I love you, too. And I'm coming home, Lexie. I promise."

His pet name for her made her eyes get wet. No one else called her Lexie. "You friggin' better." She pressed the heel of her hand to her cheek to absorb a rogue tear and, for once, didn't hate him for it.

"I'm sorry I can't make it tonight."

She tapped the phone's volume button. Adam's voice was hard to make out in the noisy bar. "You didn't just say what I think you said, did you? I'm already here."

"It's an emergency. I wouldn't stand you up if there was any way to get out of it."

Allie rolled her eyes. Everything to do with his job was always an emergency with her brother. He ought to have the word "duty" tattooed on his forehead. And whatever the issues, he was always sure he was the only person who could possibly handle it.

"Does this mean I won't get to see you before you go?" she asked, trying to mask the disappointment in her voice. It was hard though, because her throat went tight in the middle of the question.

"Of course not. Let's get up early and have breakfast tomorrow morning."

She was still disappointed, but she knew she had to swallow her emotions. She wasn't going to send him off on the memory of her being a petulant brat. It would just confirm his belief that she was still thirteen. "I'll take what I can get," she told him.

"Good," he said. "And when I say early, I mean early. Don't stay out partying all night."

Allie sighed. She shouldn't be surprised by his assumption. She shouldn't be hurt by it, either. The truth was she rarely drank anymore. Not since college, but her family had built an image of her as the crazy party girl, and arguing wouldn't change that. Angie said the only thing that would ever change it was time. The self-help book on her night stand said the only thing that could ever change it was *her*.

"Allie?"

"I'd have called it a night already if I hadn't been waiting for you." That probably sounded defensive. "I'll see you in the morning, big brother. Early."

"Night, kid," he said.

Allie tapped the end button on her phone and dropped it into her bag with a sigh. This was not how she'd pictured the evening going, but as long as she got to see her brother before he left, she'd be content.

She drained the last of her drink--rum and diet with a splash of grenadine--and decided to head back to her hotel room. Fort Sill, Oklahoma wasn't so far from home that she couldn't have made the trip back to Big Falls, but she'd vowed to do the responsible thing, and plan ahead, just in case she had a couple drinks with her brother. She wasn't about to get behind the wheel after she'd had a drink, not that her family would believe that.

What other people think of me is none of my business, she reminded herself.

Mentally reciting quotes from self-help books usually calmed her, but not when it came to her family.

She pushed herself to her feet, wobbling a little on the heels of her boots. Stupid choice in footwear, she thought. Sneakers were her usual choice, but she'd wanted to dress up for a night on the town. It had been so long since she'd had one, she'd let herself get a little excited about it. She glanced down at the skinny black jeans that hugged her legs all the way to her knee-high boots and smiled a little.

Uncomfortable, but worth it. She looked damn good.

Allie took another step, trying hard not to wobble. The rum was hitting her harder than she'd realized. She'd skipped lunch, and she couldn't remember the last time she'd had a drink. Ever since her brother in law Jeff had been killed in action, she'd been on high alert, ready to run to Angie's house any time she was needed. And she'd been needed a lot. *Thank God for our family*, she thought. And then she smiled, because she'd just been complaining about them in her head a moment ago.

Another careful step. She looked up to make sure she wasn't about to run into anyone, but as soon as her gaze left the floor, the heel of her boot caught on something. She tried to regain her balance. Her arms flailed in front of her, but it was no use. She stumbled forward and slammed into a hard chest.

A strong arm wrapped around her waist to steady her. She looked up into warm blue eyes and a face so handsome she couldn't catch her breath for a second. Everything froze, and then switched to ultra-slow motion. The handsome stranger's glass flew right over his head and crashed into the big, angry looking guy behind him. The angry guy lunged toward him, and Handsome shoved her backward out of his path. She stumbled, tripped over her heels and fell to the floor, bumping her head on a table on the way down.

"Hey!" She was too surprised to utter anything more intelligent. But it didn't matter, because the word was barely out of her mouth before the good-looking stranger crashed onto the floor, too.

His head landed on her chest and she felt a mix of embarrassment and excitement. She knew she should move, stand up, get out of there. Something. But all she could do was gape at the man lying on top of her.

His eye was red and puffy.

That big guy hit him.

It seemed her brain was functioning again at last. Allie glanced toward the bar and saw the meaty giant, beer still dripping down his face. He was advancing fast.

The man on her lap shot her a killer smile, apparently unconcerned with the brute. The puffy eye should have messed up his good looks instead of adding a rugged and irresistible appeal. When he grinned, a dimple appeared in his cheek, and a chill tap-danced up her spine.

"There are easier ways to get a man's attention," he said.

"Believe it or not, I wasn't throwing myself at your feet."

"No? Maybe I'm throwing myself at yours, then."

"Cute, but how about you get off me before you have two shiners instead of just one?"

His grin widened. Not exactly the desired effect, but she had to admit that smile was almost enough to make her forget to be annoyed with the guy.

He pushed himself to his feet and held out a hand to her. She grabbed it grudgingly and started to pull herself up when he suddenly let go again. She plunked right back onto the floor.

"Even less funny the second time," she muttered.

The big guy at the bar had finally made his way through the crowd. He was holding the front of her new friend's shirt and was about to punch him again, but a dazzling smile and brilliant blue eyes weren't her rescuer's only strengths. He dodged the blow, twisted free, grabbed her by the hand and pulled her with him toward the exit.

"I hope you're worth all this trouble," he said.

She wanted to tell him he'd never find out, but the hulk was already in pursuit, shoving people aside or plowing over them.

They pushed out through the door, into the cool March wind. It had been much warmer when she'd walked into the bar earlier. But the sun had set, and now it was raining. The temperature had dropped by at least ten degrees, and the wind made it feel even colder. Allie glanced behind them, but didn't see any sign they were being followed.

She was still a little shocked at the direction the night had taken. And he was still holding her hand.

"Sorry about your drink...and your face." She pulled her hand out of his. Her palm tingled where he'd held it. The danger seemed to be behind them, but adrenaline was still pumping through her system and she felt warm and tingly, despite the weather.

"I'm Logan," he said. "And you are?"

"Leaving." She said it fast, before she could talk herself out of it.

"That's cold. I just got decked because of you, and you're not even gonna tell me your name?"

"I'm Allie," she answered before she realized she was going to.

"Beautiful name. It suits you."

Allie rolled her eyes. "Does that line usually work?"

"Give me a break, I just got my face smashed in by Lou Ferrigno. My material is bound to be a little off."

"Only a little? Did Ferrigno scramble your brains, or are you just really bad at pick-up lines?"

Logan's eyes sparkled with mischief. "I have other assets."

That much was perfectly clear, she thought, trying to resist the urge to glance at the muscles she had felt so clearly before, when he'd been lying on top of her on the barroom floor. His t-shirt and leather jacket did nothing to hide the hard planes of his chest, and those sinfully tight jeans made her think all kinds of things she shouldn't be thinking. She forced her eyes back to his face, but his grin told her he knew exactly where her mind had been.

He took a step closer and Allie's mouth went dry.

"So, Allie, what exactly do you plan on doing with the rest of your night?"

"That, Logan, is none of your business."

He pursed his lips, as if considering her words, and Allie felt her eyes widen as he took a step closer. His body wasn't touching hers, but she could feel the heat radiating from him and it made her want to lean closer.

He raised his hand and ran it through her hair, and she couldn't think of one damn word to say. He looked at her, blue eyes penetrating.

He's going to kiss me, she thought. She knew she should be annoyed. She didn't even know him, but there was no denying the butterflies in her stomach or the goosebumps rising on her flesh. He flashed that damn mischievous smile again.

"Peanut shell," he said pulling something from her hair.

That was *not* a prickle of disappointment, she told herself. She wouldn't have let him kiss her anyway. He was a stranger, and *even she* knew better than to make out with strangers outside of dive bars.

"Well, like I said, I should get going. Sorry about…everything."

She turned and started to walk up the wet sidewalk toward her hotel. She was not using her best judgment, and probably ought to get away from this guy before she did something stupid.

"That's it? I thought after getting me punched in the face and spilling my drink, you'd at least offer to buy me dinner."

She glanced over her shoulder, but didn't stop walking. "Something tells me that's not the first time you've been punched in the face. And it's probably not going to be the last."

"True. But it might be the first time it was undeserved. I usually have it coming." He fell into step beside her.

"That part I believe. But I bet if you think hard enough, you can come up with a reason. Karma's funny that way."

Logan smiled again. "That's an interesting point. And probably true. So, no dinner?"

"Definitely not. I don't make a habit of buying dinner for strangers who follow me down dark streets in the middle of the night." Allie looked at him pointedly.

He held up his hands in mock surrender. "Am I giving off a stalker vibe? Cause I can go. It's just that this isn't the best neighborhood. And a young, ridiculously attractive person shouldn't be walking down dark streets in the middle of the night all alone."

Allie turned her head quick, but her smile was quicker. "Ridiculously attractive, huh? That's sweet, but I can take care of myself."

"I was talking about me. I've already been assaulted once tonight. Not sure I can handle another incident like that."

She couldn't stop the laugh. It bubbled up in her chest and she lowered her head as it escaped. "I see. So, you need a bodyguard?"

"A bodyguard makes me sound like a wimp. I prefer to think of it as employing the buddy system."

"I see your point," Allie said throwing him a sideways glance. "But this is my stop. Do you think you can manage the rest of the way on your own?" She glanced up at the three-story hotel where she was staying, in absolutely no hurry to go inside.

"I'm not sure. I should probably be under observation for at least thirty minutes, just to rule out a concussion. Don't you think?"

"Well, I definitely wouldn't want you to drop dead the second you stepped in your front door."

"Worried about me?" Logan asked.

"No, it's just that people saw us leave together. I'd be questioned and I have a busy day tomorrow."

Logan smiled again and that damn dimple in his cheek reappeared and made her lose her train of thought.

"There's a bar in this hotel," he said. "It's still early. I could buy you a drink to make up for the fact that you're stuck in my company for a little longer."

"It'll take more than a drink to make up for that. And I think you're underestimating your ability to annoy me if you think that will solve the problem." Allie looked up at him and smiled. She wobbled on her heels again, and this time she didn't think it had anything to do with the alcohol or the boots. He held out his arm and she took it. Oh yes, he was trouble. No doubt about it.

An hour later Allie and Logan were sitting in a corner booth at the bar. They'd agreed to just one more drink each, and it seemed neither of them was in a hurry to finish. Allie wanted to have her wits about her. Logan was too good looking, and he could charm the claws off a lobster. She didn't trust herself to make good choices around him, but she was having fun. She didn't want the night to end too soon.

It was hard to believe, but they had been talking non-stop the entire time. Conversation came easy with him. She told him about her little photo studio, and how she was carving out a living for herself doing what she loved. She told him about her house and the special place she lived—Big Falls—and how legend had it the town chose its residents. People Big Falls wanted to keep always wound up staying. And people she didn't like couldn't shake her dust off their boots fast enough. She was a living entity, Big Falls, Oklahoma. Allie told him all that, and more. She would talk until she ran out of things to say and then he would ask another question and she'd start talking all over again.

"So, you're in town to visit your brother and he stood you up?" Logan asked after another lull in the conversation.

"Not entirely his fault. He's the responsible one. Responsible people always get stuck with the last-minute crises."

Logan smiled. "I bet he wouldn't be very happy if he knew you were here with me instead."

He was looking deep into her eyes and Allie took a sip of her drink, feeling suddenly self-conscious. "Probably not, but he wouldn't be too shocked either."

"Really? So, you do this a lot?"

Allie laughed. "*No.* Never, actually. But he doesn't know that. My family is convinced that I'm only capable of making bad decisions."

"You have to admit, bad decisions are much more fun than good ones."

"I'll have to take your word on that. Contrary to what my family thinks, I've been very careful to avoid bad decisions for the last couple of years."

"And why is that?"

Allie took a slow sip and thought about her answer.

"When I was a kid, I think I just craved attention. When we were younger, my sister was always the brainy one, and my brother was the star athlete, and I didn't really have a *thing*. So, I became the troublemaker. But then everyone's lives got crazy. My brother was gone all the time, and my sister lost her husband. I was needed. So, I stepped up. I *grew* up. But it's hard to get my family to see that," she sighed. "How about you? Are you the doting son or the black sheep?"

The smile disappeared from his face.

"Let's not talk about my family."

"Why not? Is it that bad?"

"I don't want you to think I'm telling you some sob story just to get sympathy." He smiled again, but the sparkle was gone from his eyes and Allie found herself wishing it would come back.

"You don't need my sympathy." Allie inched closer to Logan in the round booth.

"Why's that?" Logan asked. The sexy smile returned to his face. The dimple reappeared and Allie let out a sigh.

"You made those bad decisions sound like so much fun, I think I might want to try one."

Logan leaned in close and his fingers twined in her hair. His lips brushed across hers and her mouth tingled. He pulled back a little, looking at her, waiting for her to react.

She knew what she *should* do. She *should* run back to her hotel room, bolt the door and sleep until this particular bad decision no longer seemed like a good idea. She stared into Logan's deep blue eyes and knew that wasn't going to happen. All her common sense was gone.

She smiled and raised her lips to his. She pressed her body closer. He kissed her, soft and sweet. His lips were warm on hers, gentle and tender. But she didn't want tender. Not tonight. She wanted something to make her forget her sister's broken heart, her nephew's shattered childhood, and the gaping whole Jeff's death had left in their family, to make her forget how it was tearing out her heart to see her brother leave them from the same airport, heading for the same destination.

As if reading her mind, Logan turned his head, angled his mouth across hers and kissed her like she'd never been kissed before. A tingle of anticipation swirled in her stomach. She didn't want to feel sad or afraid tonight, and she knew that if she let him, Logan would keep her too busy for any of those thoughts to enter her mind. He could make her forget, for a little while. If she let him, he could make her forget. And that was exactly what she was going to do.

She placed a hand on his chest, pushed him gently backward and said the first thing that popped into her head. "Wanna walk me to my room?"

CHAPTER TWO

MAY 30TH

The camera flashed and the tiny naked baby scrunched her face a little tighter. Allie tried to suppress a yawn. Why the heck was she so tired? She'd always been a morning person. Even when she was a kid, she'd bounce out of bed at the crack of dawn, ready to start the day. Not lately, though. She'd been tired and groggy every day until noon. She wondered if she was depressed.

Her one-night stand had become her favorite daydream. She'd been fantasizing about Logan for weeks, and enjoying it too much to try and break the habit. It wasn't just about the amazing sex, either. Sure, it was sometimes. A *lot* of the time. She relived that night in visceral snippets every time she closed her eyes. But there was more. She'd tried casting other leading men in those fantasies. Movie stars, country male vocalists of the year, all the usual suspects. But it didn't work.

It wasn't the sex. It was him. There was something about him that had twisted itself around her and wouldn't let go. She could not stop thinking about him. And the image she saw most often in her mind was his face. His sexy smile, his killer dimples, and those Elvis-blue eyes.

Somehow, she still hadn't convinced herself that tryst in a hotel room with a stranger had been the biggest mistake she'd ever made. It felt more like a moment on a paradise island in the eye of a hurricane.

Her practical mind, the one that had been created by her mother, told her she was lucky he hadn't been a serial killer. Hadn't she seen enough made-for-TV movies to know how flings with strangers could turn out?

But he wasn't a serial killer. He was just…wonderful.

That night had been healing for her. Logan seemed to sense whenever worry nipped at the edges of her mind, and he'd grab her eyes with his and just hold them, and the worry would go away. For those few hours, she'd stopped mourning Jeff and worrying about Angie. She'd stopped bleeding for Cassie, who was walking now, and Jack, first-grade paleontologist, who'd lost their daddy. She'd stopped wondering if her big brother was going to make it back home.

Logan had stopped everything. He'd made it easy, looked at her as if she was the most beautiful woman he'd ever seen, touched her as if he could read her mind, held her as if he didn't want to let go.

And it had felt like she'd hit a reset button.

She'd been doing better, since then.

It had been her first one-night stand. Her only one-night stand. But some part of her had really expected him to call her afterward. That was probably stupid, and maybe naïve.

She was embarrassed now, that she'd written her phone number on a slip of paper and slid it into the pocket of his jeans. She didn't want to be that girl. The one who thought a one-night stand was going to lead to a relationship. Allie was too smart for that. And yet every day since, those fantasies just kept spinning out. And the memories, replaying. And her pulse sped up whenever the phone rang.

But he hadn't called.

So far.

Obviously, the night hadn't been as amazing for him as it had been for her. She shouldn't be suffering such crushing disappointment.

Maybe that was why she felt so tired and run down. Maybe it was just from getting her hopes up so many times and being disappointed. Maybe she ought to try convincing herself that Logan was an arrogant ass. A handsome, sexy, arrogant ass who just happened to be crazy good in bed and even better at turning on the charm. Faking a real connection. Making a girl like her believe there was more going on than sex.

But none of that had anything to do with her client, so she stifled a yawn and tried to snap a few more pictures while the brand-new baby on the pillow in front of her was willing to cooperate. She adjusted the light and snapped some shots from another angle.

The baby stretched and made a face that reminded her of a grumpy old man, and she zoomed in and captured the moment.

Newborn shoots were hard. Babies didn't always cooperate. Parents' expectations were high and, to be honest, she wasn't a huge fan of working with kids. Sure, they were cute—even this one. He would grow into those ears. However, she was an artist, and you couldn't create art when you were rushing to get through the shoot before the kid started whining, wailing, pooping, or puking. She'd only agreed to take the shots as a favor to her sister. Apparently, the mother didn't get along with Edie, the other professional shutter bug in town. And Edie was a saint. She'd helped Allie get into the business, sent clients her way when she needed down time. If her sister's friend didn't like Edain Brand Armstrong, there was something wrong with her.

She aimed to catch another cute expression from an angle that minimized those ears and clicked the shutter. The new mom, Janet Slater, pushed her way into the frame just as the camera flashed, ruining yet another shot.

"His face looks oblong from that angle. And I don't think there's enough light."

"That might be because you keep stepping in front of the spots," Allie said as gently as she could manage. It was taking superhuman effort to keep from biting the woman's head off and she wondered if it was PMS.

J-Slate gave her a dirty look. "You might as well start taking pictures of me holding him. All these have been absolutely hideous."

Allie took a deep breath and counted to eight. She'd been shooting for ten. "You should put a diaper on him. He's been uncovered for a long time." The studio was warm, but in her experience with babies, scant though it was, she'd found twenty minutes naked to be well inside the red zone.

"I showed you magazine photos I liked. We're going for an upscale look. That's the whole reason I came here instead of going to Walmart. Now can you take the pictures or not?"

"I *can*." She tried not to growl the loaded reply.

Janet smoothed her blond cigar curls and picked up her infant. Allie was feeling bad for the little guy already. His mother was probably already planning which extra-curricular activities he would participate in, where he was going to go to college and what careers were worthy of him. She tried to pose them as best she could, even though momzilla clearly thought she knew better and contradicted Allie at every turn.

It took another ten minutes just to get the first shot set up. But then she was finally ready and snapping shots, changing angles, snapping more. The mother tried her best to look serene and hide her bitchiness. It didn't work. Medusa trying to play the Madonna.

The baby started to stir. He wiggled in his mother's arms and turned his head from side to side.

Allie said, "Um, I think he's—"

"Take the pictures!" Janet snapped.

The little guy turned his head back toward the camera and smiled the tiniest smile Allie had ever seen. The camera flashed, Janet shrieked and the baby relieved himself. And not in the better way.

Allie's stomach heaved. No warning, whatsoever. Maybe it was the heat or the mess or exhaustion, but whatever it was, there was no stopping it. She pulled the camera strap from around her neck, grabbed the first thing she could reach and doubled over, retching in agony.

When it was over, she felt hot and lightheaded, but other than that, she was completely fine.

"I guess we should call it a day," she said wiping her mouth. She looked down and realized she'd just thrown up in Janet's designer diaper bag. "Don't worry about the sitting fee."

The furious mother gathered up her baby and headed for the restroom. She didn't take the diaper bag.

"Alexis Wakeland, if you were hung over, I swear on your life, I will never send another customer your way as long as you live."

The censure in her sister's voice didn't surprise her. Neither did the fact that she had instantly believed whatever crazy story Janet Slater had told. Angie was the oldest in the Wakeland Clan and she took her role seriously. She took *everything* seriously. Since her husband's death, that tendency had grown even stronger.

Jeff had possessed the rare and magical ability to make Angie mellow. Without him, her crazy ran wild and no one could get it back in check.

Allie rolled over on the studio couch and tried to ignore her sister. It didn't matter what she said, Angie was going to believe what she wanted to believe. And most of the time, she chose to believe that Allie was a screw-up. For a while, Allie had earned the title. She'd got into trouble in high school. At fourteen, she'd been caught joyriding with seven friends crammed into the science teacher's VW Beetle. He'd parked outside a middle school dance with the keys in it. She and her pals hadn't been able to resist. Allie had driven, and a cop had pulled them over. There'd been open containers in the car, sickeningly sweet strawberry wine coolers. The cops hadn't cared that she'd been the only one *not* drinking them.

At fifteen she'd cut school to hang out with her boyfriend under the highway bridge, where the Cimarron River twisted lazily by. They'd had a cache of junk food and a pack of Marlboros. He'd also had a whole box of condoms, but she didn't know that until later, when his dad and her mom showed up. His dad grabbed him and shook him, and the condoms fell out of his pockets like rain.

At sixteen she'd sneaked into Mrs. O'Connor's classroom and stolen the final exam, answers and all, ran off copies, and returned it. It'd never occurred to her how suspicious it would look when she and her friends all got perfect scores.

She'd spiked the punch at the Honor Society reception. She'd organized a kegger for senior skip day. She'd switched college majors five times and then dropped out.

One day she woke up and realized that all she was getting out of college was a permanent hangover and a pile of debt. She could pursue photography without it. She'd taken plenty of courses on it. And she was good.

Since then, she'd taken charge of her life, like all her self-help books said she could. She'd bought a house, a car, and started her own business, a business that had its own green-and-white striped awning on Main Street. But her older siblings still saw her as the irresponsible baby of the family who broke curfew every weekend.

She'd given up trying to prove she was anything else.

"Allie!" Angie demanded. "I didn't come over here just so you could ignore me. Now, answer me. Are you hungover or is there something wrong with you?"

"I'm not hungover. I haven't had a drink in months. I don't do that anymore, Angie." She sighed and rolled her eyes. "Maybe I have food poisoning or something."

The little girl on Angie's hip babbled and cooed, happily unaware of her aunt's misery.

After giving the floor a quick once-over, Angie set Cassie down on her bottom. The toddler didn't stay put for long. The second her mother let her go, she pulled herself to a standing position and tottered unsteadily across the studio.

"Glad I cleaned that up," Allie muttered. Thankfully, the backdrop behind and under Janet and her baby had caught all the mess. It was now occupying a trash bag out back, with one designer diaper bag for company.

Angie perched on the edge of the studio's little couch and placed a hand on Allie's head. "You don't have a fever. You look pretty terrible, though."

"Thanks, Sis," Allie said with a hint of sarcasm. "I don't think your friend is going to be back anytime soon."

Angie shrugged. "I'm pretty sure we're not friends anymore."

"Uh-oh. Why?"

"She was being mean. So, I told her she shouldn't get pictures done until her baby grows into his ears."

Allie laughed and then instantly regretted it. "Don't make me laugh. I don't want to do to your purse what I did to her diaper bag."

"I heard. That was a Gucci, you know."

"Yeah. I'll have to send her a check. So what was she being mean about? What did she say?"

Angie sighed. "That you were either hungover or knocked-up and she wasn't sure which was scarier."

"That's ridiculous," Allie said, but the second the words were out of her mouth, alarm bells started going off in her head. She closed her eyes, trying to remember the date of her last period. "No. It's gotta be food poisoning. Morning sickness can't possibly be this bad or women would never reproduce." She could hear the edge of panic underlying her attempt at humor, and she knew Angie heard it, too.

"Allie, is there a possibility that you *could* be pregnant?"

Allie shook her head. She was being paranoid. She and Logan had used protection. She couldn't be pregnant. "No." But now that she was thinking about it, she was pretty sure she hadn't had her period in the last month. Not since that night, in fact. *Hell.*

"I don't think so." She glanced at Angie and saw the look on her face. The one she always got when she thought Allie was messing up her life.

Rolling her eyes, Angie reached for her purse. "I picked up a test kit on the way over. Just in case." She pulled out a plastic bag with the Big Falls Pharmacy logo on the front.

"That is the most insulting—God, Angie, do you really think I'm running around having sex with every man I meet?"

"Of course I don't think that."

"I've had sex once this year. Once!" *Well, more than once. A lot more than once. But all in the same night.*

"Okay." Her sister looked sorry. But then she said, "And when was that?"

She pressed her lips tight, still mad. "The night before Adam shipped out."

"That was in March," Angie said, nodding. "So, you'd have noticed if you'd missed a period in April."

"Sure I would." She blinked, thinking back, and realizing she didn't remember. "I don't really write it down or anything. It's not like I'm having so much sex I have to keep track."

"And how about this month? Did you—"

"Not so far, no."

"It's the thirtieth, hon." Sighing, Angie held out the kit again.

Allie wanted to be mad. She wanted to be outraged, but a little voice in her head told her to stop being self-righteous and take the damn test. It wasn't going to be positive. She couldn't be pregnant. The test was going to be negative and then she would laugh at herself for even being paranoid enough to take it in the first place.

She managed to sit up without hurling on something, even though her nerves had her feeling more nauseated than ever. Clinging to what was left of her pride, she took the test kit from her sister, and walked across the studio to the small bathroom to follow the instructions on the package.

The results were supposed to take a minute to show, but before Allie had even finished washing her hands, she saw the little plus sign starting to appear. It was faint and fuzzy. She rubbed her eyes and hoped she was imagining it, but the longer she looked, the clearer it became and by the time the minute was up, the plus sign was as clear as day.

Angie's knock on the door startled her. She must've jumped a foot in the air. "Allie? Are you okay?"

Allie pushed open the door and stared at her big sister, knowing she was about to prove herself the biggest screw-up who'd ever lived.

"I'm pregnant," she whispered. Saying it out loud made it so much more real. Suddenly she was picturing herself carrying a newborn, holding a little pooping, puking infant and not being able to give it back when it started crying.

"Who's the father?" Angie asked.

Allie closed her eyes and a tear managed to work its way out of the corner of her eye. "Logan. I didn't catch his last name."

The look on Angie's face was incredulous. "Alexis!"

"Oh God, please don't tell Adam. He's going to kill me."

CHAPTER THREE

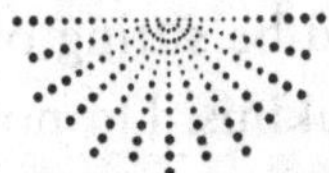

DECEMBER 19TH, 6 DAYS BEFORE CHRISTMAS

Sgt. 1st Class Logan Edwards stood at the Will Rogers International Airport and waited for his luggage to make its way around the carousel. He was feeling antsy. Not because of the luggage or the crowd of people around him, but because he was home. Back in the States after spending nine months in a dry and dusty wasteland. And he felt more out of place here than he ever had there.

He looked around him. There were families everywhere. Mothers and fathers with happy children and impatient babies waiting to be reunited with the missing members of their families. Hundreds of people filled the space, but not one of them was there for him, and he doubted anyone ever would be.

It wasn't that he felt sorry for himself. He didn't. He was used to being a loner. Growing up in foster care, he'd learned to depend on himself. Other people would let you down. He didn't *do* family, or holidays. And he was only this uneasy was because he was about to do both. For some inexplicable reason, he had ignored his better judgment and agreed to spend his mid-tour R&R and worse, with Captain Adam Wakeland and his entire family.

Adam was also his best friend and his commanding officer, which had made it pretty tough to say no.

He was smiling at him as he came across the floor. He'd *been* smiling ever since they'd set foot on U.S. soil. Actually, he'd been smiling for the entire week before they'd left, and it was really starting to creep Logan out.

"You know," Logan said, "we could've gone anywhere in the world for R&R. We could be sitting on a beach, drinking beer and looking at girls in bikinis. I'm not sure Oklahoma City is gonna beat that."

Adam's smile widened. "We're not staying in Oklahoma City. My family lives north of there in a little town called Big Falls. And my mother would kill me if I skipped a family Christmas."

"Big Falls? I've heard of that." The name was familiar. He didn't know why, but it wasn't the kind of name you would forget.

"Nobody's heard of Big Falls," Adam laughed. "I'm *from* there and I barely know where it is."

Logan shrugged. "So, you're saying we're not likely to find a beach or pretty girls in bikinis?"

"No beaches. Pretty girls, sure, but my sisters are off limits," Adam said. And it was funny how his smile turned into a scowl when he said that, and how he emphasized it by catching Logan's eyes and turning up the intensity of his stare.

"Got you. No hitting on your sisters. You think I'm stupid or just suicidal?

"Let's hope neither."

He gave an exaggerated salute. "Yessir, Cap."

Adam's features relaxed again. And then that smile popped back into place like it had become his face's default setting.

Logan figured he was Adam's polar opposite on the family front. Adam was a devoted son, a protective brother, and the pride of his small hometown. He relished being an uncle to his sister's two kids, whose dad was KIA a while back. IED on a road he and Adam traveled themselves a couple of times a week.

Adam had been married once, but he didn't talk about that. He was everything that Logan would never be. A brother, son, uncle, husband.

"It's not too late to change our minds. We could buy tickets on the next flight to Tahiti. Or maybe Fiji?"

"Forget it," Adam said. "I told Mom you're coming. There's no escape for you, Sergeant."

"Sergeant first class," he corrected. His rucksack finally emerged through the carousel's rubber eyelashes. Logan grabbed it and waited. After a few minutes, the carousel stopped spinning and Adam sighed. His bag had not appeared.

"I swear they lose my stuff every time. I'll be right back." He walked toward the help window and Logan swung his own bag onto his back and headed over to one of the many sets of dark glass doors to look out at the Oklahoma skyline.

The night sky was clear and full of stars. It looked calm and peaceful and it made him feel even more out of place. He wondered if it was too late to change his mind. Christmas with a big family had never been his idea of fun, but he and Adam had been through a lot while they were deployed. They'd saved each other's asses more than once, and when Adam asked him to come home with him for the holidays, it had sounded like a great idea. It might be a chance for them to hang out without death and danger looming over their heads.

Now that he was here, though, he was having doubts. He wondered if he could fake a family emergency and sneak off to a hotel for a couple of weeks. Probably not, since Adam knew he had no family and no one else who would call him for help. He wished he'd never spilled his life story.

It was too late now. He was stuck, and he was just going to have to make the best of it.

A woman pushed through the glass doors in front of him,

and ran into him at full speed. He didn't even have time to side-step. The force of their collision sent him reeling backward, but he maintained his footing. Her purse flew out of her hand and Logan caught her by her elbows to keep her from falling. For a little thing, she sure packed a wallop.

"You okay, miss?" he asked.

She lifted her face, and everything in his brain stood still. It was her. It was Allie, the woman he'd been fantasizing about since the day he'd left U.S. soil.

"Allie?" he whispered.

She stood there for a second, blinking back at him. Recognition lit her pretty eyes, then disbelief chased it away, and then they got all jittery in what looked an awful lot like panic.

For the first time since he'd left Afghanistan, Logan wasn't forcing a smile he didn't feel. This one was real.

He had convinced himself over the past few months that she couldn't really be as beautiful as he remembered her. He thought he must have amplified it in his mind, the way he must've amplified the night they'd spent together. There was no such thing as sex that good. But seeing her in front of him, he realized that she was even prettier than his memory had painted her.

Before, he hadn't noticed the golden strands in her dark chestnut hair or the way her long, dark eyelashes framed those warm brown eyes. The sparkle in her eyes was brighter than he remembered. Her face was softer, her hair was longer, but she was still stunning. She was wrapped in a long, shapeless peacoat that hid the rest of her body, but thinking about what was underneath that coat made his pulse pick up speed.

He wondered what he should do. It had been a one-night stand. A mind-blowing, phenomenal one-night stand, but a one-night-stand nonetheless. It wasn't as if they really knew each other. But all the same, he imagined pulling her into his arms and kissing her like the soldier and the nurse in that famous Times Square photo.

The increasing look of panic on her face made him think that probably wasn't the best idea. She wasn't here for him. That much was obvious. What if she was waiting for a boyfriend or fiancé? He didn't like the way that thought made him feel.

First things first, he needed to let her go. That would be a good start. Logan took a step backward and reluctantly dropped his arms to his sides and hitched up his bag.

Allie snapped her mouth closed, apparently over the initial shock. "It's you," she said.

"Do you tackle every man you meet? Or is it just me?" he asked, trying to ease the tension.

Her smile was forced and nervous. "I guess you bring it out in me. You never told me you were military."

"You never asked."

She shifted uncomfortably, and her eyes darted around the baggage claim area. With a small pang of jealousy, he wondered who she was looking for.

"How have you been?" she asked. She kept her tone light, but she couldn't keep the stress from showing in her eyes, and he took pity on her. Running into a one-night stand was awkward enough without feeling like you had to make small talk.

So, even though he'd have liked to get reacquainted with the subject of his fantasies these past nine months, he decided to let her off the hook.

"You don't have to do this," he whispered, leaning in a little closer. "It was a one-time thing. There's no reason you need to make small-talk with me now." He should have left it at that, but part of his brain was reliving the details of that night and he couldn't stop himself from leaning in a little closer and adding, "Unless you're interested in making it a two-time thing?"

She glared at him so intensely he thought the ends of his hair might start smoking, and damn if it didn't make him grin even more.

"You know lines like that are probably why you get punched so often," she told him.

"That has crossed my mind a time or two."

But Allie didn't say anything else. She had spotted something behind Logan and her expression changed again. The anger was gone, replaced by a look of sheer happiness. Her entire face lit up, and Logan felt another pang of jealousy. She smiled so brightly that she was practically beaming. He turned around to see who had caused the change in her.

"Adam!"

By the time Logan caught sight of his friend, Allie was already hurrying through the airport and throwing her arms around him.

The feeling in his chest was indescribable. Jealousy was back, and it was huge, but then he felt a moment of intense panic, wondering if Allie and Adam were a couple. Had he slept with his best friend's girl?

He shook that thought off the second it entered his head. If Adam had a girlfriend at home, he'd have mentioned her. The only thing about home that he didn't like to talk about was his ex-wife.

Logan considered that possibility for a moment; could Allie be the ex?

No, Adam wouldn't be this happy to see his ex, whom he'd described as a cold, heartless shrew who'd served him with divorce papers the day he got home from a deployment without a word of explanation.

Logan didn't know Allie very well, but he couldn't imagine her doing anything like that.

And then it snapped into place and his heart sank. Adam was hugging her, and it wasn't a passionate hug, it was the hug of a protective brother. He thought he might be sick, because it was obvious that the insanely gorgeous woman he'd been dreaming about for months, the one he'd talked to his commanding officer about, at length and occasionally in far too much detail, was Adam's kid sister. And if Adam found out about their night together, Logan was pretty sure he wouldn't have to worry about spending Christmas with the Wakeland family. He might not have to worry about celebrating another Christmas at all. Ever.

The hug ended, and Logan wondered if Allie had already told her brother about him, because the look on his face was one of shock.

"Lexie, what the hell?" Adam grabbed her shoulders and held her back a little, glancing down between them.

Logan was confused. Her name was Allie. Not Lexie.

Adam had gone from grinning like an idiot to looking like an Tomahawk had just detonated nearby.

Allie glanced nervously at Logan and then back at her brother. "Can we do this somewhere else? Somewhere less public?"

"I'm not going anywhere until you tell me what's going on."

Allie licked her lips and her eyes darted toward Logan again. "Isn't it obvious? You're going to be an uncle again." She pressed her hands to her belly--a very expanded belly. The coat had masked it somewhat, but Logan had no idea how he'd managed to overlook *that*. He felt suddenly ashamed of himself. He'd just propositioned a pregnant woman. Not his finest moment.

It was a good thing the baby's father wasn't around to put him in his place.

That thought made his heart hurt. It wasn't that he wanted a relationship with her. He was only home for two weeks, but he had to admit that when he saw Allie, he'd been hoping they could at least have a repeat of their amazing night.

But obviously, she'd found someone else while he'd been away, and by the look of her, it must be pretty serious.

"Lexie, why didn't you tell me about this? I want details. I didn't even know you were seeing anyone." Adam was clearly flustered, and Logan felt like he was eavesdropping on what should have been a private conversation.

"There's lots of time for that, but it's a long story, and I don't feel like relaying it in the middle of a crowded airport. So how about we get out of here?" Allie kept glancing in his direction.

It seemed strange at first, but then Logan realized that she had no idea who he was or why he was still standing there looking at her like an idiot.

Adam seemed to come to the same realization at the same time. He looked at Logan, as if he'd just remembered he was there. He shook his head like he was trying to clear the fog. "Sorry, man. Lexie, this is my buddy, Edwards."

"Uh, Logan Edwards. Nice to meet you. Lexie." Logan tried to let her know he wasn't going to give away her secret. Their secret.

Her mouth dropped open for a second, but she recovered quickly. "It's Alexis, actually. Adam's called me Lexie since I was born. Mostly because I hate it, but everyone else calls me Allie." She smiled through a clenched jaw and shook his hand.

He closed his around it, small and warm and soft. His palm tingled. He wondered if hers did too.

"Edwards is going to stay with us for Christmas, Lex. Sorry, I didn't get a chance to tell you sooner, but I know how you are about the holidays and figured you wouldn't mind."

Allie's perfectly constructed mask slipped momentarily and Logan could see the devastation hiding behind it. But only briefly. She schooled her face into the frozen smile of a department store mannequin.

He felt bad for her. He couldn't imagine having to sit around the Christmas tree with Allie and the man whose baby she was carrying. It would be awkward for him and probably a hundred times more awkward for her. And the possibility of Adam finding out what he'd done with his little sister was enough to make Logan break out in a cold sweat. It would be better for everyone if he got out of here while he still could.

"You know, Adam, I think I might just grab a hotel room. Looks like you and your family have a lot of catching up to do." He shifted his bag higher on his shoulder. "Allie, congratulations and good luck with the new baby." He gave her a reassuring smile, but that didn't seem to comfort her. In fact, she was looking at him as if he had two heads.

"Logan's not used to dealing with family drama," Adam said.

"You don't come from a big family, Logan?" Allie asked.

"Not really."

"He comes from no family," Adam said. "Logan made the mistake of telling me he's never had a family Christmas, and I knew you and Mom would never forgive me if I didn't bring him home to Big Falls to fix that."

Big Falls, right. That's where he'd heard of the town before. Allie, that night, that magical town she'd talked about. And suddenly she was looking at him like she might look at a lost puppy. Oh, hell.

"I still think my plan to spend Christmas relaxing under a palm tree in the tropics would have been just as good." He said it just to fill the silence stretching out between them.

"You'll have plenty of chances to check out hot girls in bikinis. But this might be the only chance you'll ever have to try my mother's world-famous Christmas dinner. Come on, Edwards. Nobody should be alone at Christmas. Right, Lexie?" Adam looked at her for support and Logan was sure he wasn't going to find it. There was no way she wanted him around when she had so much else going on.

But Allie surprised him. She nodded and gave Logan a half-hearted smile. Warmth spread through his chest at the sight of it, because it was genuine, even if it wasn't full blown. "Adam's right. No one should be alone at Christmas. You're welcome to spend it with us." Her voice cracked a little when she said it.

"I don't want to intrude. You have family stuff going on."

Adam punched him in the shoulder, hard. "Lesson one about families: there's always family stuff going on. We made a plan and I'm not letting you blow it off. You're coming home with us."

He knew he shouldn't. He should grab a hotel room or jump on the next plane that would take him far away from here. He should spend the next two weeks on a beach enjoying the company of some beautiful woman who would make him forget all about Allie Wakeland once and for all. That was what he was going to do, but when he opened his mouth to say so, he found himself agreeing to stay instead.

"Good decision." Adam smiled and put an arm around his sister, steering her toward the nearest exit. Logan followed, wondering if this experience was going to be harder for him or for Allie.

"So, I'm going to be an uncle again," Adam said as they headed for the exit. "What do I get? Another niece or another nephew?"

"I don't know. I want to be surprised," Allie said.

"I can't believe you kept this secret. How did you convince Mom and Dad not to tell me?"

"I told them I'd move to Hawaii and take the baby with me if they told you before I had the chance. I thought this needed to be an in-person kind of conversation."

They had walked out the door into the chilly December air and Allie pointed out the car parked in the front lot.

"Is that because I'm not going to like the father?" Adam asked. He'd been trying to keep his tone conversational, but there was an underlying edge to it. "He hasn't married you yet, I take it?"

"Nope."

"You haven't told me much about the guy."

"I haven't told you anything about the guy."

"That bad, huh?"

Allie glanced at Logan and a prickle of apprehension tickled the back of his neck. It was weird that she hadn't at least mentioned her boyfriend to her brother. They were close. That seemed like the kind of information they would share. But then again, pregnancy seemed like something she'd have shared with Adam him, too.

Unless…unless there *was* no boyfriend. An icy finger traced a path up his spine. He shivered in reaction. What if she'd gotten pregnant during a one-night stand with a complete stranger?

He spent a minute counting in his head the exact number of months he'd been gone. The number of months it had been since he'd been with Allie. Their night together had been in the middle of March. He did a quick count in his head. Nine months.

Panic rose inside him, and he tried to push it down. It was almost exactly nine months. He didn't know much about pregnancy or babies or any of that, but he didn't think she could be up and around if she was nine months pregnant, could she? Women didn't drive around picking people up at airports when they were that close to giving birth. Did they?

It couldn't be his. She must have gotten pregnant after he'd left.

Instead of bringing relief, that thought stung. He hadn't stopped thinking about her in all this time. Apparently, she'd got over him in a hurry. But that was a good thing, right? Because that meant things shouldn't be awkward. At least not *too* awkward.

The notion calmed him down a little. Sleeping with his C.O.'s sister was one thing. If Adam found out about that, he'd kick his ass all the way back to Afghanistan. But knocking her up? That would be even worse. If he had been responsible for that one, Logan was pretty sure he'd go missing and no one would ever find his body.

Captain Adam Wakeland was an intimidating man. Logan wasn't afraid of him, but that was because he had no reason to be. He and Adam understood each other. They'd become best friends.

He didn't think the man who knocked up Adam's sister was going to fare very well. Not unless Adam decided he was worthy of his little sister, and from what he knew about Adam, he doubted many people would pass that test.

"I'll take the bags," Adam said. "Lexie, go ahead, get in and relax."

Logan handed over his bag. Ordinarily he would have argued and insisted on helping, but he wanted a second with Allie.

She climbed into the driver's seat and fired up the car and Logan climbed into the back. From the speakers, Bing Crosby promised to be home for Christmas.

"Listen," Logan began, and Allie turned around to look at him from the front seat. He swallowed hard but hurried on. "I don't want you to worry. We don't have to tell your brother or anyone else about that night. I'm not gonna ruin whatever you've got going with…you know, the guy. The baby's father." He gave her what he thought was a reassuring smile.

Allie pinched her nose between her fingers, lowered her head, and blew out a long breath. "Were you dropped on your head as a child? Or did that guy at the bar cause brain damage after all?" she asked after a long pause. The trunk slammed and Adam started walking around the car. "It's your baby, you idiot."

Logan was stunned into silence. And then Adam was opening the door. "Want me to drive, Lexie?"

"It's fine."

"Are you sure, cause I can—"

"It's fine. Get in."

Oblivious, Adam climbed into the front seat and cranked up the volume a little. "I love this song," he said and then he was crooning along.

Logan's heart clenched so hard he thought he might be having a heart attack. He took a deep breath and the pain let up, but his pulse pounded at a rate that was much faster than usual and he was sure Adam and Allie could probably hear it from the front seat. He wanted to tell her that was impossible. To ask if she was sure. He wanted to ask how the hell any of this could be happening when he had worn a condom every damn time they'd had sex that night. He wanted to dive out of the car and run into traffic on 281-North, because he was pretty sure he had a better chance of surviving being hit by a semi at full speed than he did of surviving Adam's wrath when he found out the truth. But he didn't do any of those things; instead he sat in the back seat of the compact car, and tried to imagine himself with a baby in his arms.

CHAPTER FOUR

*A*llie punched her pillow and tried for the hundredth time to fall asleep. Sleeping during pregnancy hadn't yet been easy. She almost always felt dead on her feet by dinnertime, fell into bed for a few hours only to wake up for good by 3 a.m.

This time, the things keeping her awake were different. It wasn't the impossibility of finding any comfortable position, or the worry about her ability to be a single mother.

This time, every time Allie closed her eyes, she saw Logan. She remembered the night she took him to her hotel room in vivid detail. She could still remember the smell of his cologne and the feeling of his razor stubble against her face when he kissed her. She remembered his smooth hard chest and the calloused texture of his strong hands as they ran over her body.

And then she'd remember what an ass he was at the airport and it would cancel out the rest.

She ran her hands through her hair in frustration and gave up on going back to sleep. Why did it have to be him? And why did he have to show up now and throw her entire world into upheaval? At Christmastime?

She was going to have a baby in a matter of days, and the last thing she needed was more anxiety in her life.

Footsteps sounded in the next room. It would eventually be the nursery, but at the moment, it was occupied by Logan Edwards. Adam had claimed the den, downstairs because it had a TV. It would have looked odd if she'd argued against that arrangement.

Logan was up and pacing. She shook her head, thinking about that. About Logan in the next room surrounded by her baby's stuff.

His baby's stuff.

She felt a little bad for him. She was sure this wasn't the way he'd pictured his homecoming. He'd probably imagined another bar, another girl, another night of crazy sex with absolutely no consequences. *For him.*

She sighed. She hadn't wanted him to find out about his impending fatherhood like this. She was planning to tell him. She'd tried to find him when she'd realized she was pregnant, and when that hadn't worked, she'd called Adam's ex-wife Riley. Riley was a private investigator who did not live in Big Falls, which was a plus.

Riley was good and she was discreet. She was also still on the case. Allie supposed she'd better call her and let her know that her ex had dragged home the object of her manhunt.

Allie had thought that by the time Riley tracked Logan down, she'd have figured out the right way to break the news to him. And you better believe the right way wouldn't have included the phrase, *It's your baby, you idiot.*

The baby kicked her hard.

"I might not have got off on the right foot with your dad, peanut." She rubbed her belly and the baby kicked again. She had started trying to interpret the baby's kicks, and she was pretty sure this one was telling her to go and fix things. There was no sense waiting to talk to him. They were both awake in the middle of the night worrying about it. Better to pull the bandage off quickly, right?

She forced herself to sit up, which was more of an effort than she cared to admit. Her movements couldn't be described as graceful these days.

She'd seen a video once of an elephant that had flipped onto its back and couldn't manage to roll over again. She was pretty sure she looked similar to that. She pushed over onto one side, trying to gain enough momentum to roll upright. It took a couple of tries, but eventually, she managed it.

She crept across the floor, as quietly as an elephant can creep, and out her bedroom door. There, she waited, listening for noises that would tell her if her brother was awake downstairs. That was the *last* thing she needed. Adam used to sleep like a rock, but his time in the Army had changed that.

Allie's home was a two-story farmhouse just off Main Street. She had bought it at a foreclosure auction a year ago, and ever since, she'd been working to fix it up and make it her own. Her bedroom and the nursery/guest room were on the second floor. Adam was staying downstairs in the den. She used to have her studio set up in there, but this year she'd rented space on Main Street. Excellent location near the park, super convenient for outside shoots.

She listened carefully. There were no sounds from the first floor, and she was reasonably sure that even if her brother was awake, he wouldn't hear her tiptoeing around upstairs. If he did, she'd just tell him it was one of her nine thousand nightly bathroom trips. *Ah, the joys of pregnancy.*

She paced to Logan's door and stood there for a minute, trying to get the nerve to knock. Her stomach flip-flopped and her brain started trying to talk her out of this. It was the middle of the night. This conversation should be saved for the light of day. She knew those were all excuses, that she was really just chickening out, but she didn't care. She hadn't even thought about what she was going to say. And obviously winging it wasn't working for her. This had to be planned and done right.

Then the door opened and she was standing face to face with the man she'd been thinking about all night. Hell, for the past nine months.

His dark hair was wet and as tousled as a military haircut could get, which meant that it was lying flat in some places and sticking up straight in others. His blue eyes were darker than usual. That playful sparkle was gone, and without it, they were the color of midnight. He looked tired and worried.

She had the crazy urge to smooth his hair, to run her hand along his freshly shaven cheeks, but following urges like those was what had got her into this mess in the first place.

"Want to talk?" he asked.

All thoughts flew from her head. He'd taken a shower and the smell of his body wash hung in the air, clouding her brain and making her remember the last time she'd been close enough to smell that woodsy scent.

She cleared her throat and tried to ignore the fact that her face felt as hot as the surface of the sun. "Unless you'd rather wait. I understand if you're too tired or something...." Her voice trailed off.

"I couldn't sleep anyway." He held the door open and she stepped inside. It felt weird. The once-cozy nursery seemed suddenly foreign. He'd only been occupying these walls for a matter of hours, but the room no longer felt like it belonged to her.

She crossed the floor and sat down on the edge of the futon. There was no point in small talk. They both knew what this discussion was about. She took a deep breath, and began. "I know this must be awkward for you, Logan. I didn't expect to see you tonight, and I never intended to just blurt out the news like that. But it is what it is."

Logan crossed the room and sat down on the other side of

the open futon, but he didn't say anything. The blankets were still strewn across the mattress, a clear indication he'd been tossing and turning as much as she had.

She didn't want to look at the bedding, didn't want to think about the fact that she was sitting a foot away from the bare-chested, sexy man who had fulfilled her every fantasy just a few months ago. And every night since. So instead, she kept talking.

"This must be a shock. I don't blame you if you're knocked for a loop. I was too when I first realized we'd made a baby. I've had time to get used to the idea but you're still in the early stages. I imagine you have questions. I had a thousand."

He cocked his head to one side. "I can only think of one, at the moment. Are you sure it's mine?"

She stared at him, blinked twice. "Ouch."

"I'm sorry. That's offensive. Rude. But on the other hand, I barely know you, and—"

"I'm sure it's yours." She didn't give him details. He didn't need to know her entire sexual history. Not that the list was that long. All he needed to know was that he was the father.

The expression on his face told her he wasn't convinced. He couldn't doubt her word on this—could he? "If you have something to say, just say it." She was getting angry.

Logan pursed his lips, considering his options. "It just seems...convenient."

"Are you friggin' kidding me? *Convenient?* I'm pretty sure if you had an eight-pound human sitting on your bladder and kicking your kidneys twenty-four-seven, you might not think *convenient* was the best description--"

"I just mean, we only had sex once—"

"Six times."

"Seven, if you count that...um, but what I meant was, one night. We were only together one night. And we used condoms. It just seems...*unlikely* I got you pregnant. That's all."

"This was a mistake," Allie said.

Logan nodded and the look on his face was so condescending that she wanted to slug him. "I thought so."

She glared at him. "No, you moron. Trying to talk to you, *that* was a mistake. Inviting you to stay here, *that* was a mistake. You don't seem to have the brain capacity to understand your role in all this, and that's fine. Until you showed up today, I was prepared to do this entirely on my own, and that plan hasn't changed."

Logan held up his hands in mock surrender. "Hold on, you told me to tell you what I was thinking. That's all I was trying to do."

"Yeah, well, I didn't realize you were thinking stupid things."

He smiled. "Do you realize how many times you've called me stupid in the last six hours?"

"Do you realize how many times you've *been* stupid in the last six hours?"

"Give me a break. I've been awake for a day and a half, and the first person I recognize on American soil tells me I'm about to become a father. It's a lot to process."

She took a deep breath and blew it out. This day hadn't been easy for him. And it was probably natural that he'd doubt her. In his defense, she did hop into bed with him in record time, so he probably had no reason to think it wasn't a regular occurrence for her. Not that she should be finding excuses for him. The man was infuriating. She took another breath and willed herself to get through the rest of the conversation and get it over with.

"If you could try not to call me a liar for a few minutes, that would probably help the conversation along," she said.

"I never called you—"

"First of all, as I've already pointed out, we had sex more than once. A lot more."

"Yeah," he said. A lopsided, absent smile pulled at one side of his mouth. "I didn't even know it was possible to have that much sex in one night."

"Secondly," she said, trying to keep herself on track, "we did use condoms, but one must have broken or something because, here we are. And third, our *evening together* was on March twenty-ninth. Which means my due date is tomorrow."

"Tomorrow?" he looked at her with eyes as wide as the full harvest moon.

"Yes. Tomorrow. But Doc Sophie says I'm not showing any signs of impending labor yet. First babies tend to go past the due date."

"Wow."

"So, you're right that it's statistically improbable that during the one night we were together and using condoms I would get pregnant. But there wasn't anyone else, Logan. Not for a long time before and not since. And it's even more improbable that I'd run into you nine months later, on the eve of my due date. And it's really freaking crazy that you turned out to be my brother's friend who also just happens to be spending the holidays in my baby's nursery. But guess what? It's all true, so there it is."

He didn't argue anymore.

"I don't have anything to hide, Logan. Order a damn paternity test once the baby's born, and find out for yourself. Or you know, don't. Don't have the test done. Don't believe me. It doesn't matter. I don't expect you to be involved anyway."

For the first time since she'd told him the baby was his, he seemed like he might believe her.

"So...what do we do?" he asked.

"*We* don't do anything. You hang out for the next two weeks and pretend everything is normal. I'm going to do my best to get this baby out of me and that's it. My plan hasn't changed. I don't want, need or expect anything from you. I just thought you deserved to know." She had been staring at the floor. Intentionally not looking at him. But she chanced a glance in his direction. The look on his face was hard and unmoving and she wondered if he was back to not believing her.

"What makes you assume that I wouldn't want to be a part of my kid's life?"

Allie shrugged. "I don't know. Maybe the fact that you've been trying to deny it's yours ever since I told you. Or maybe just that you were trying to pick me up five minutes after we met. And when you saw me again at the airport, you went right back there. How do you expect to do that with a baby on your hip?"

"You didn't exactly make the pick-up that much of a challenge. Don't start judging me for things you actively participated in."

Allie suppressed the urge to growl. But barely. "I was just trying to say, you don't have to feel responsible. You don't have to be involved. You *definitely* don't have to tell Adam. He never has to know. I've prepared for this. I can do this on my own."

"Are you done?" Logan asked. His voice was tense and she could tell he was clenching his jaw. It wasn't what she'd been expecting. He looked like a man facing his executioner, determined, resolved and ready to accept his punishment.

"Yes. I'm done."

"Good. What the hell is wrong with you?"

Allie's eyes widened. "Excuse me?"

"You just assume that I have no problem lying to my best friend? That I have no problem sitting here for the next two weeks, watching you carry my baby while I pretend that I had nothing to do with it? You assume that I'm going to cut and run just because you tell me it's okay?"

"Oh, I'm sorry, did I somehow misconstrue the last fifteen minutes of this conversation? You know the part where you were calling me easy and saying the baby isn't yours? Suddenly, I'm the bad guy for trying to give you a way out?"

"So shoot me for not wanting to be conned into claiming a

kid that isn't mine. But *if* this is my baby, there's no way I'm going to abandon it."

"Fine. You seem to have all the answers. What do *you* suggest we do?" Allie shifted on the futon and tried to hide her exasperation.

"Well, for starters, we come clean. We tell your brother the truth."

"No!" She jumped to her feet. Jumped being a relative term.

"I'm can't lie to my best friend, Allie." He stood up, too.

"Fine," she said. "You go tell my brother that you may have knocked me up, but you won't be sure until you get a paternity test, because you're pretty sure I indulge in casual sex with too many men to be clear about it. And then go back into a combat zone with him. I *dare* you."

A look of worry shadowed his face. It was only there for a second, but she knew she had him.

"Adam will be pissed. There's no getting around that."

"Adam will be furious," she corrected.

"But he's a good soldier and a great friend. He'll get over it."

"Yeah, right after he kills you."

He shook his head. "I have to tell him."

"Uh-uh, mister. This is *my* baby, *my* brother, *my* life, and *my* house you're standing in right now. We're doing this my way, Logan."

"It's *our* baby," he said softly.

"What happens when you get sent to your next base? What happens when you have to move halfway across the country or across the world and *our baby* doesn't get to see you anymore? You might not abandon this baby on purpose, but we both know in the long run, that's exactly what would happen. I don't want my child to have to face that kind of heartbreak." And she didn't want to face it herself.

He sighed, pushing a hand through his hair. His eyes were

dark and sad and Allie felt guilty for causing it. "People make it work. We could make it work."

"We?" She almost laughed at the word. "How?"

"We could get married."

The baby kicked hard. Allie sank onto the futon again, because her knees sort of gave out at Logan's words. "I thought you were going to stop saying stupid things?" She sat there stunned, one hand on her belly.

"It's not stupid. It's a good idea. Maybe the only idea. You're a self-employed photographer, right?"

"What the hell does that have to do with anything?"

"Well, that doesn't really come with a guaranteed income, does it? Do you have health insurance? Maternity leave?"

"I buy my own insurance, and I have some money saved. I'll make it work." Honestly, her savings were pretty small, and her health premiums were breaking the bank and would go higher once the baby came. It had been something she'd been worried about for a while, but it was hardly a reason to chain herself to someone for life.

"If we got married, you would have all that. You'd have a housing allowance to help pay your mortgage, and insurance for you and the baby. Are you really prepared to do this on your own?"

If she was honest with herself, she wasn't. She was absolutely terrified. Who wouldn't be? She was the family screw-up. She was the one who dropped out of college. She was the one who failed chemistry twice and only passed the third time because she was dating her TA. She was the one who always, always had to be bailed out of tough situations.

No. That was the old me. I'm not that kid anymore and I haven't been in a long time.

She didn't *want* to be bailed out this time. She wanted to do this on her own. For her child. "Are you really prepared to give up life as you know it and become a family man?" she asked, because that seemed like the reality check he needed to snap him out of his idiotic suggestion.

A look of terror crossed his face and she said, "That's what I thought."

"Do you have a better plan?"

"A better plan than marrying a stranger? Yeah. Anything but that." Allie closed her eyes. "My plan is the same as it's been since I realized I was pregnant. I'm going to have a baby and raise it on my own and do whatever it takes to make it work. I see no reason that needs to change just because you showed up. Two weeks from now, you'll go back to Afghanistan and I'll go back to my life and we'll pretend this never happened."

He shook his head slowly. "Whether you marry me or not, I'm not going to walk away from my child."

"Do you really want the responsibility of raising a baby?" Her tone was sharp, even to her own ears.

"You don't know me. So don't act like you do. What were you expecting from me? Relief? Gratitude at being let off the hook?" His tone was icy and the look in his eyes matched it.

"I know more about you than you think," Allie said. She hadn't put two and two together. Not until now. Adam had talked about his friend Edwards several times, and none of those conversations made her think that Logan was an aspiring soccer dad. "Adam's told me all kinds of stories. I just didn't realize they were about you until now. Responsibility and stability don't seem to be in your nature. You're too busy charming women into jumping in bed with you."

"Don't forget that you were one of those women."

"How could I forget?" She looked down at her belly. "I'm the one living with the consequences." Her eyes pierced his. She felt like she was playing chicken, and he didn't look like he was going to back down.

"There are two things I never do. I never walk away from my responsibilities and I never lie to my friends. So yes. Whatever the consequences are, I'm going to face them. So, are we planning a wedding or not?"

"I wouldn't marry you for all the gold in Fort Knox. I'm *definitely* not going to do it for health insurance and a housing allowance." Allie took a deep breath and tried to be logical. "What's my favorite color?"

Logan looked confused. "I don't know."

"What kind of music do I like? What's my best friend's name? Which side of the bed do I sleep on? You don't know anything about me. You have no idea if we'd be compatible."

"If memory serves, you prefer the left side of the bed, and in that area, we seemed more than compatible."

Allie blushed. "That's not enough for a marriage."

"It's a start."

"Military marriages are impossible. Adam and his wife couldn't make it work, and they were the most perfect couple I've ever seen. My sister Angie and her husband—" Allie's eyes clouded with tears just thinking about it. "They were barely holding it together and then he deployed and didn't come home, and now she's raising two kids by herself. Even when you have something amazing to start with, there's no guarantee. We'd be starting with nothing. I'm not willing to take that chance, and I can't believe that's my best option. Not for me and not for my baby."

Logan's face was hard as stone. "*Our* baby, and I can't think that the best option is for me to abandon my child. I'm not willing to do that. Not ever, and I'm not willing to lie to my best friend, either."

"You're both going to be gone for the next three months. What's the point in telling him now?" She held up both hand, palms up. "You can't tell him, Logan. I'm not ready for Adam to know."

If Adam knew, Allie was sure he'd be thinking exactly the same thing that Logan was. He'd be pushing marriage and he'd use guilt. He'd tell her to *do it for the baby*. It was off the table. She might not know exactly what she wanted out of life for her and her child, but she knew what she didn't want. She'd always known she would never marry a soldier. She'd said it a thousand times. Never, never, never.

"Then you need to *get* ready," Logan said, interrupting her thoguhts. "Adam's my best friend. I realize that will probably end the second I tell him, but I'm not comfortable staying under the same roof as him and keeping this a secret. Much less spending the next three months with him in the desert, pretending I'm not the guy."

"God forbid *you* do anything that makes you uncomfortable. You self-centered short-sighted, morally superior *prick*." She wanted to storm out of the room. She was *trying* to storm out of the room. In her head, she was already slamming the door in his face, but in reality, she was struggling to get off the futon. It would have been funny if she wasn't ready to rip someone's head off. Preferably Logan's.

The hard expression on his face gave way to a tender smile, and he held out a hand to help her up. She slapped it away and pushed herself up to her feet, one side at a time, and straightened slow, holding back the groan of pain pushing up from her back.

"Like I said, I can handle the consequences on my own." She strode out of the room, barely resisting the urge to slam the door behind her, because Adam would hear it downstairs. Once in the hall, she sagged a little, pressed one hand to the small of her back and rubbed hard. Leaning on the wall, she took a few nice deep breaths. Very unsatisfying way to storm out of an argument.

The spasm in her back eased a little. She was afraid of bringing it on again, so she only *tiptoed* angrily back to her own room.

She didn't know how she was going to sleep.

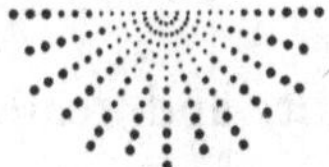

Morning sunlight filtered through the curtains, waking Logan from a restless sleep. For a minute, he wasn't sure where he was. Birds were singing outside the window. The bed was warm and reasonably soft and the smell of bacon filled the air. He sure as hell wasn't in Afghanistan.

He opened his eyes and reality came crashing in. A heavy weight settled on his chest and for a second, he felt like he couldn't breathe. He was in Allie's house. Allie was pregnant. He'd made a child with his best friend's sister. He was going to be a father.

He thought back to the conversation he'd had with Allie a few hours earlier and wished he could believe it was just a bad dream. He'd acted like an ass, and then asked her to marry him. Insulted her, then proposed to her.

"God, what was I thinking?"

Allie surprised him though. She did the opposite of what he'd expected and offered him an easy out; a chance to pretend that none of this was happening.

That was exactly what he'd wanted. At least it was, until

she'd handed it to him. Then he'd panicked, and proposed in a knee-jerk reaction. Marriage was a *terrible* idea.

He should probably be relieved she'd said no.

Said no, my ass. She practically ran from the room.

In his mind he saw her again, struggling to get up off that low-slung futon, belly first. She'd smacked his hand when he'd tried to help. She had to rock to one side to get momentum. His lips tried to smile.

He pressed them tight, and realized her rejection stung. Why, he wondered? Her reaction shouldn't come as a surprise. He'd known his whole life that he would never have a family. His parents gave him up when he was a kid, and he'd bounced around the system. A couple of good foster homes, a couple of really bad ones. He'd made a conscious decision not to get too attached to anyone.

He hadn't had what you'd call a girlfriend in his entire adult life. He didn't even really have friends. Not until he'd joined the Army. It had never bothered him, it was more like a condition he knew he had, a part of his DNA. He accepted it as who he was.

But now Allie seemed to think his own kid—their kid— would be better off without him. Pain seemed to radiate from the center of his chest, an area he'd kept cool and dark and quiet all these years. It was swollen and pulsing now.

It hurt knowing she believed that. It hurt even more that part of him agreed with her.

He pushed through the wave of unfamiliar emotions and sank his feet into the sands of logic. Feelings wouldn't do him any good. He had bigger issues right now than what Allie thought of him.

He had to tell Adam.

The thought made his stomach drop. He wasn't afraid of Adam, even though the guy had four inches and fifty pounds on him. Logan could handle himself in a fight, but he had no desire to fight his best friend. The captain was the closest thing to family Logan had, the only person he'd allowed to get close.

Dammit, he should've known better.

He'd spent most of the car ride yesterday trying to remember every detail of his night with Allie, searching for any way he could have realized she was Adam's sister. The name had thrown him. Adam always called his sisters Angie and Lexie.

Big Falls, though. That might've tipped him off. She'd mentioned Big Falls. But he wasn't sure if Adam ever had before then.

Still, sleeping with your buddy's sister was a huge violation of the bro-code. Getting your buddy's sister pregnant was even worse. Add in the fact that Adam was his C.O. and this was the biggest shit storm Logan could imagine. And he had to clean it up.

That was where his focus ought to be. Not on letting little Allie Wakeland hurt his feelings.

He yawned, still tired. He'd barely last night.

The guest room was also the future nursery. His visit was a surprise to everyone, so he didn't imagine there had been time to put all the stuff away somewhere else. Allie had apologized when she'd led him into a bedroom full of baby stuff, most of it still in its original packaging. Logan had been hoping he could shut himself in a room, forget his problems and sleep until he came up with a solution, but that was hard to do while he was staring at a boxed-up crib. A crib that his own little boy, or little girl, would sleep in. The front of the box was a full color photo blown up huge, the crib all assembled with the softest looking little baby sleeping inside.

Something swelled in his chest again.

He sighed, threw his legs over the edge of the futon, and thought about Allie. After their fight, she'd gone back to her room, but she hadn't slept, either. Logan had heard her moving around, through the thin bedroom wall.

He had been angry at first, at the situation he thought he didn't want, and then at her for wanting to do it without him. The anger had been good. It made him feel like he could get through this. He was used to existing in a continuous state of Logan-against-the-world. He was used to fighting. He tried to hold onto his anger, tried to be glad she couldn't sleep. But he couldn't quite manage it.

Then after a while, he'd heard something else. No more pacing. She was crying, and he knew it was his fault. No matter how shocked and how angry he'd been, that didn't give him the right to make things harder on her. Geeze, she was carrying his kid. What was the matter with him?

He should go to her, he thought.

No, he shouldn't. She was angry, and every time he opened his mouth, he made her angrier. He needed to give her some space.

He grabbed his bag from where it lay on the floor, next to a box with a space-aged container and the words Diaper Genie across the front. What the hell was a Diaper Genie? He pictured Barbara Eden nodding her head and making a dirty diaper disappear in a poof of pink smoke.

He looked around at all the contraptions and equipment. How could he be a father? He didn't even know what most of this stuff was.

He picked up a tiny shirt that resembled a straightjacket. The shirt wrapped around and snapped on the sides and the sleeves folded over on the ends to form mittens. He had no idea why a baby would need mittens.

Her due date was tomorrow.

She said there were no signs yet, but still, he didn't have very long to get used to the idea. Much less bone up on baby-care.

He should get going on that.

But first he had to tell Adam. God, it made him sick to his

stomach to think about that. Maybe he could wait until after the paternity test.

"You're an idiot, Logan," he whispered. He didn't need a paternity test. In his heart, he knew that. Allie didn't want his help. She had no reason to lie to him, nothing to gain. Besides, her eyes didn't lie. He never should've said the things he had to her.

None of this was easy or fair. Not to either of them.

He sighed and laid the baby straightjacket back in the box of clothes, wishing he had trusted his better judgment and stayed in Afghanistan. But there was no point feeling sorry for himself. This was a new day. He was who he was. He had to do the right thing. He had to tell Adam.

Logan got dressed. When he opened the bedroom door, the sounds of voices floated up from downstairs, along with the smells of bacon and fresh coffee. He walked down the stairs into the brightly-lit living room. A little girl with curly blond hair and chubby legs was running unsteadily, chased by a little boy who looked about six or seven. Toys were strewn around the floor at their feet. The little girl tripped over a teddy bear and landed on her face. Before Logan could react, the little boy was picking her up and setting her back on her feet, and without missing a beat, she giggled and took off running again.

He felt out of place. Allie's house was full of noise and people and laughter.

The living room opened into a small dining room. The kitchen was on the other side of a wide island. Adam was sitting at the dining room table with two people who must be his parents. The man looked like an older version of Adam, except that his build was smaller and his face was narrower. He had the same wide brown eyes, though.

Allie had those eyes. All dark brown like melting chocolate.

The woman at the table didn't resemble either of her children. She had a tiny frame, dyed-red hair in a big curly mop, and bright blue eyes that beamed with love as she gazed at Adam, who sat in the chair beside hers. She had one tiny hand over his bigger one on the table and she was telling him what sounded like local gossip he'd missed. Two of the McIntyre boys had apparently got married. One had a little girl, and the other a newborn, and someone named Vidalia was over the moon with joy about her newest grandbabies.

Logan moved through the place like a ghost who didn't belong. Allie stood at the kitchen range talking to another woman. She glanced his way when he walked into the room. Her gaze was so cold it almost froze him in his tracks. He shouldn't have been so harsh last night. He didn't want her to be his enemy.

Sighing, he went back to the table and sat down in an open seat across from Adam, who greeted him with a warm smile he didn't deserve.

"Mom, Dad, I want you to meet Logan Edwards. Edwards, Beth and David Wakeland."

Adam's mother stood up, hurried around the table and wrapped his shoulders in a big hug. "Welcome home," she said. Adam's dad held out a hand and gripped his firmly.

The woman in the kitchen came to the table with a stack of coffee mugs and set them around. "And I'm Angie, Adam's big sister. The two little monsters running around here are Jack and Cassie."

Angie looked nothing like Adam and Allie. She had straight blond hair and her blue eyes matched her mother's. She was taller than Allie and so thin she looked like she might break. Despite the smile on her face, her eyes were unspeakably sad. It was no surprise. Logan knew her husband Jeff had been taken out by a roadside bomb while driving in a convoy. It had been a year or a little more, if he remembered right. Adam had talked about his brother-in-law a lot. He'd loved the guy. Grieved him hard.

Angie held out a thin hand and Logan took it and gave a gentle squeeze. He could feel her bones under a cool layer of skin. Then when he let go, he said, "Thank you all for letting me spend the holidays with you. You're a beautiful family."

"We're happy to have you," Beth said. "But won't your family be upset that you're not home? If Adam tried to get out of Christmas with me, I'd never let him hear the end of it."

"I don't have anyone to upset, Mrs. Wakeland." Logan said it with a carefree smile and braced himself for the reaction that always followed that statement, the awkward pity.

"You call me Beth," she replied, and instead of avoiding the topic the way most people did, she asked, "Have you been on your own for long?"

"As long as I can remember."

"Well, that means you're free to spend holidays with us from now on. We've got enough family to go around."

Allie stepped out of the kitchen with the coffee pot and started filling the cups on the table. Her expression told Logan she might not be thrilled about her mother's invitation.

"Thank you for opening your home to me."

"Don't thank us. This is Allie's home," Beth said. "Dave and I downsized a few years ago. With just the two of us, we couldn't see maintaining a big old house any longer."

He remembered Allie telling him that night that her family thought she was a screw-up. She'd changed, but they couldn't see it, she'd told him.

He bet her pregnancy hadn't helped her cause.

She filled his coffee cup and set it roughly on the table in front of him. Coffee sloshed over the sides.

Logan knew he shouldn't, but he couldn't hide his grin. That display of temper was unexpected, and he found it entirely amusing. Allie glared at him and stalked back into the kitchen.

"How did you manage to get on Allie's bad side already?"

Adam asked. "I thought I was the only one who could piss her off that fast."

Logan shrugged and said the first thing that popped into his head. "I asked her if she was having twins."

Adam let out a bark of laughter.

"In that case, you're lucky that coffee didn't wind up in your lap," Angie said, stifling a grin. She followed Allie into the kitchen and returned with heaping plates of food.

Once the kids were seated at the table, the only spot for Allie to sit was next to Logan, and he worried that she was going to stab him with her butter knife. But instead, she doted on her niece and nephew and ignored him completely. He tried to pay attention to the conversation going on around him.

Adam's father, Dave, talked about the upcoming Christmas Eve celebration at The Long Branch saloon, and how they'd added something special this year. Then with a loaded look at the kids, he said, "More on that later."

Angie and her mom talked about Angie's new house just west of Big Falls. Logan overheard enough to understand that they'd had to move out of base housing after Angie lost her husband. Six months was the maximum time a family could stay in base housing after a soldier died. He glanced at Angie's kids and sighed, thinking of they'd been through.

He saw Angie spot the sympathy in his eyes, and she quickly said, "It ended up being a blessing in disguise, though, getting kicked out of base housing. I bought one of the only places I could afford, out in the middle of nowhere. Then the town purchased the huge tract of land beside it to build a reservoir. It's just a hole in the ground now, but in a couple of years, my house will be lakefront property."

"Somebody's looking out for you," he said. And she kind of beamed at him, so it must've been the right thing to say.

The family breakfast was the most noisy, chaotic meal Logan had ever seen. There was so much talking he kept forgetting to eat. A lot of the time, several of them were talking at once and yet they all seemed to get every word of it. The topics changed so fast he could barely keep up, even when he was focusing. Often, though, his attention wandered to Allie.

She was discussing dinosaurs with her nephew, Jack. The boy spewed information like he was livestreaming a paleontology website. How did a seven-year-old retain so many details?

"The ankylosaurus is my favorite," Jack said, "It has a giant club for a tail, and armor all over its body."

Allie said, "My favorite is a triceratops. It looks like it's wearing a crown. Now *that's* a dinosaur with some great fashion sense."

Jack laughed. "It's not a crown, Aunt Allie. It's a bony frill, and it was probably used for defense against predators." The little boy suddenly turned to Logan. "What's your favorite?"

"I...um...a pterodactyl?"

Jack rolled his eyes. "That's not a dinosaur."

"Of course it is. Pterodactyls are the flying ones that turned into birds."

The little boy slapped his forehead in an overly dramatic show of disbelief. "First, they're *not* dinosaurs. They're flying *reptiles*. Second, they're actually called pterosaurs, not pterodactyls. And third, even *big* dinosaurs evolved into birds. Like the t-rex."

Logan looked at the kid in surprise. "Seriously? What kind of bird did the t-rex turn into? An ostrich? Or an eagle? Something big and scary, right?"

Jack shook his head. "My book says the closest bird to a t-rex is actually a chicken."

"No way. There's no way a t-rex evolved into a little tiny critter that we serve up fried with a side of biscuits. That can't be true."

"It's definitely true. Right, Aunt Allie?"

Allie nodded. "I'm pretty sure that's right. I read him the book."

"A chicken? That's amazing. How'd you get to know so much about dinosaurs, Jack?" Logan asked.

"I read a lot. Mom says it makes you smart. You should try it. You can borrow some of my books if you want."

Allie made a choking sound and covered her mouth with a napkin. But he could see the smile in her eyes, and for just a second, was dazzled by it.

She cleared her throat, took a sip of water, and said, "It would take an awful lot of books, Jack," she said softly.

The little boy laughed. "Yeah. You might have to read all the books at the library."

Logan smiled. "T. rex didn't read any books, and it worked out for him, right?"

"Not really. He turned into a chicken!" Jack giggled.

"And now we're eating his eggs for breakfast. Guess that's not such a good thing."

"*He* couldn't lay any eggs," Jack said. "Only girl chickens can lay eggs. You really gotta read some books."

Allie laughed along with her nephew and her eyes met Logan's for the first time since she'd sat down. The force of her smile made him feel warm all over, like he'd just sipped a hot coffee after a freezing desert night, and he couldn't pull his gaze away.

"Don't let this guy fool you," Adam said from across the table. "He's actually one of the smarter people I know."

"You must know a lot of dummies, Uncle Adam."

That brought a round of laughter from everyone, including Logan, but Jack's grandfather didn't look amused.

"Where are your manners, young man? Sergeant Edwards is soldier, just like your daddy was. Show him some respect."

At the mention of his father, the little boy's smile disappeared. He could see the regret on Angie's face instantly.

"Sorry, Sergeant Edwards," Jack said.

"Don't worry about it, kid. Truth is, I got punched by a real big guy a few months ago, and I think he knocked some of my brain cells lose. But who needs brains when you have a face like this." He winked and Jack managed a weak smile.

Allie gave him an appreciative look and that damn warmth flooded his body again. He didn't know what that was all about, but he intended to get to the bottom of it. It was probably some kind of chemical reaction that made cavemen willing to fight off saber tooth cats to protect their pregnant cave women, ensuring their children would be born. It probably happened to all human males when a woman who was carrying his baby smiled at him.

His baby. The thought made his heart pick up its pace again.

"May I be excused?" Jack was already out of his chair.

"Me, too!" the toddler said. Angie nodded, letting her little girl slide off her lap. Jack followed his little sister into the living room and after a minute the noise of rambunctious play filled the silence.

"Okay, Allie, I think I've waited long enough." Adam turned his attention to his sister. "You said you'd give me all the details in the car last night and then you barely said two words about this whole...situation. So, it's time. Who's your new guy? And what exactly does he intend to do now that you're-- " Adam paused as if he was searching for the right word.

"Knocked-up?" Allie supplied.

"I was gonna say *with child*, but that, too. Who's responsible for this?"

Allie rolled her eyes. "I'm responsible, Adam. Just as much as anyone else." Her eyes darted to Logan's, and he knew she was nervous he was going to tell Adam right then.

"You know what I mean, Allie. When did you start dating? How long have you been together? Do I know him? Do I hate him? Is that why you didn't tell me?"

Allie took a deep breath. "I'm not dating anyone."

"Did he break it off? Was it because you're pregnant?" His eyebrows came down hard. "I'll kick his freaking—"

"No, Adam. There was nothing to break off."

"But if you weren't dating…?"

Logan could see the exact moment that the words sank in. Adam's face turned red and his forehead creased.

"Who did this to you?"

"It's no use, Adam," his father cut in. "We've all asked her. She won't say a word about it."

Logan cleared his throat. He was dreading this, but now was as good a time as any.

Allie grabbed his leg under the table and squeezed. The strength of her grip was enough to shut him up momentarily.

"I don't *have* to say a word," she said. "This is my life. I can make my own decisions, and I've decided I can do this. I don't need anyone's help." She was on the defensive, but Adam didn't back down.

"Allie, come on. You shouldn't have to do this by yourself," Adam said.

"There's no reason I can't. Angie does, and she's doing an amazing job."

Angie looked down at the table. "It's true. You're perfectly capable."

"Come on, Ang. You don't believe that," Adam said. "You have no choice but to raise the kids on your own. Allie does. She's just a kid. She's going to need help."

"I'm not a kid. I'm twenty-four years old. By the time you were my age, Adam, you'd already been married and were cruising towards divorce. No one gave you a hard time about your choices."

"There's a big difference between me at twenty-four and you at twenty-four."

Allie glared at her brother, but he didn't stop.

"I didn't say anything when you changed your major six times. I kept my mouth shut when you dropped out of college and opened up your *studio*. But I can't keep quiet and watch you make another mistake."

"My *studio* is doing so well I'm turning clients away," she said. "And nothing I've done in last three years has been a mistake."

"Dammit, Lexie—"

Logan cleared his throat, drawing Adam's irritated gaze. Allie gave him a pleading look and her hand squeezed his leg a little tighter. He placed his hand over hers, hoping that the action would be reassuring. He might not agree with Allie on much right now, but he wasn't about to sit there and let her be attacked for something he was responsible for. "I'm sorry, Adam." He paused choosing his words carefully. "I know it's not my place, but I don't think you're giving your sister the credit she deserves."

Adam shot a glare his way. "This isn't your concern, Logan."

"I get that. This is your family, but it seems to me like you're letting your past with your sister cloud your judgment. I'm an outsider, so I can give you an unbiased view of things. It looks to me like Allie's doing okay for herself. She's living in a nice house. She's driving a decent car. She's feeding all of us this morning. She's giving us both a place to stay while we're home on leave. Seems to me that whatever she's doing is working out pretty well. Maybe you should give her the benefit of the doubt."

Allie met his gaze and he could see the gratitude in her eyes.

"You're right. It's none of your business," Adam snapped.

"Look, Adam," Allie said. "Whether the father is involved in his child's life is between me and the father, and telling you isn't going to help either one of us make those decisions. If he's going to be around, I promise, you'll know who he is. If not, it really doesn't matter. But mainly, Adam, it's just none of your business." She looked around the table. "And that goes for all of you."

Her tone brooked no argument and without another word, she pushed back from the table and started clearing dishes.

Logan stood up and followed suit. Adam didn't look happy, but he also didn't look like he was going to press his sister any further. At least not at the moment.

"Whoever this guy is, he better have a damn good excuse for not being here," Adam whispered.

His father nodded, and Logan looked from older face to younger face, and wondered what they would think of him when they learned the truth.

CHAPTER SIX

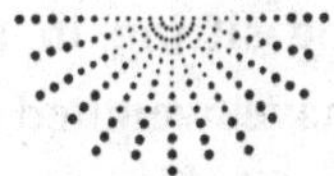

*L*ogan sat across the table from Adam and his father
feeling like a complete and utter fraud. The OK Corral
wasn't exactly what he'd been expecting when Adam
told him they were going out for a drink. It was a bar for the
locals, clean and efficient, but not fancy. The woman behind the
bar was short and curvy, with black hair shot with silver all
piled up on her head, a ready smile, and mischief in her eyes.

He thought he might really like this place, if he wasn't sitting
across the table from his best friend, who was trying to work
out who had got his baby sister pregnant.

Adam took a slow pull from his long necked brown bottle.
"We can figure this out," he said. "She might not want us to
know, but it's a small town, and we know everybody in it."

His father didn't look convinced, a fact that made Logan feel
a whole lot better. "Your sister's stubborn. If she doesn't want to
tell us, she's not going to."

"You can't be serious, Dad. She needs help. She might be
twenty-four, but on the inside, she's still a kid. She has no idea
what's in store and there's no way she can get through this on
her own. You know that. Remember the dog?"

David nodded with a sad expression on his face. "I remember."

"What dog?" Logan could not possibly *not* ask.

The men exchanged a look. David leaned back in his chair, and pointed at Adam with the neck of his beer bottle.

"It was a few years ago," Adam said. "Allie was still living at home. One day, Mom and Dad came home and there she was with this giant, filthy dog sitting in the middle of the living room. The thing must have weighed two hundred pounds. I don't know where she got it, but she was completely unprepared. She didn't have food or a leash or dog dishes. When I got to the house, she was feeding the thing hamburger out of one of Mom's casserole pans."

"Your mother was *livid*," David said, smiling at the memory.

Logan could picture it in his mind. Allie cooking up a gourmet dinner for a mutt she'd found on the street. She had a big, soft heart. "What happened to the dog?"

Adam shrugged. "It tore the house apart every time she left it alone. I don't know what happened to it, but after a week it was gone." He sighed. "She thought she could handle that one on her own, too."

Logan tried not to cringe, imagining Allie dropping the dog off at a shelter or leaving it on the side of the road. She didn't seem like the type of person who would do that. Her heart was too big. But he didn't really know anything about her.

"How's she gonna raise a child if she couldn't even handle a dog?" Adam asked, shaking his head and sipping his beer.

"People can change, Adam." Logan said it without thinking first. "

David nodded. "Allie might not be the most level-headed girl, but she's come a long way, Adam. She was only nineteen when she brought that dog home. She's grown up. You haven't been around enough to see it, but she has. That studio of hers is doing all right."

Why was Logan feeling all puffed up with pride on hearing that?

"Besides," David went on. "Your mother made me promise I wouldn't get into the middle of this, and that I wouldn't let you, either. I gave her my word. And you know better than to cross her." He shrugged. "Besides, it's not like there's anything we can do about it anyway. She's an adult. What are we going to do if we do find the guy? Force her to get married?"

"That'd be a start. Right after I beat him into the dirt for getting my baby sister pregnant and then deserting her."

Logan cringed. He wanted to come clean. At the same time, the part of him driven by the instinct of self-preservation wanted to make sure Adam *never* found out the truth. "Maybe the guy has a good excuse."

"Like what?"

"Maybe he doesn't know."

Adam sighed and tossed back the rest of his beer. "You don't understand small-town life. Everyone in this town knows everyone else's business. There are no secrets here."

"There's been a lot of gossip and speculation, but no one in town has any idea who the father is," David interjected.

"What was the speculation?"

"Nothing worth mentioning."

"Come on, Dad. I just want to know what people are saying. Small-town gossip can hurt. Allie's going through enough."

David sighed. "A few people mentioned Ethan Wyatt. He went on a few dates with your sister last winter, but it didn't amount to anything. Carter Avery's name came up, too. He spent some time at the studio getting pictures of his boys done. Nothing romantic happened between them, but people saw his car at your sister's a few times right before she let the cat out of the bag." David shrugged. "Like I said, it's nothing worth mentioning. Best if we just leave it alone."

Adam scratched his chin, looking like he wasn't entirely convinced. "Maybe I need to have a talk with Ethan and Carter."

"Absolutely not," David said. "Listen to me, son. I want to know who fathered my grandchild as much as you do. I want to find out why he hasn't been here. But interrogating half the town is only going to embarrass your sister. She doesn't need that stress. You know better than anyone how dangerous that can be. Keep your mouth shut and leave Allie alone." He tossed some cash on the table, squeezed his son's shoulder and headed for the door. "See you at the house later," he said on his way out. "Afternoon, Vidalia," he called before he left.

"Afternoon, Dave. You have a baby yet?"

"Not yet. Due date's today."

"First ones are always late," she told him "Don't hold your breath."

He left and she went back to wiping down the bar.

The look on Adam's face had changed. He didn't look angry anymore; he looked ashamed and Logan wondered what had just happened between father and son. *You know better than anyone how dangerous that can be.* Had he had a baby? Had he lost one? There weren't too many other ways to interpret David's words.

Adam drained his beer and ordered another one. For the next hour, Allie's big brother drank like someone with a reason to. He didn't do much talking, and Logan spent most of the time in his own head, trying to figure out the best time to tell his friend the truth. Now was definitely *not* it. Not while Adam was slowly getting wasted. Not in the middle of a very public place. And not in a place where everything they said and did would immediately be reported back to Allie.

That comment about stress had made Logan think. He had no experience with pregnant women, but if stress was dangerous, didn't he owe it to Allie to make her life as stress-free as he could until the baby came? There wasn't much else he could think of to do for her, but that, at least, should be easy.

"See that guy out there?" Adam suddenly broke his silence, pointing to a tall, lanky fellow standing outside the bar's wide windows. "That's Ethan Wyatt."

Logan shook his head. "You heard what your dad said. Allie only dated him a couple times."

"Allie doesn't tell Mom and Dad everything. It wouldn't be the first time she dated someone without them knowing. In high school she dated a kid for six months after telling us all they had broken up. The guy was a loser. And Ethan's no better. I always hated him."

Logan considered that for a second. He stared at the tall man with the easy smile, who stood outside the bar, and wondered if Allie'd had some kind of relationship with him. The thought made his stomach roll and he recognized the feeling as pure, green jealousy. He shouldn't feel it, he didn't know why he was feeling it, but he didn't have time to ponder it, because Adam was out of his seat and crossing the barroom towards the door.

Logan caught up fast, catching the door before it had time to swing closed.

"Hey, Adam. Welcome home," Ethan Wyatt said. "How's your sister?"

Adam didn't even respond. Instead he swung a big fist at Ethan and knocked him flat to the ground.

Logan's jaw dropped. In the five years he'd known Adam, he'd never seen him start a fight. Sure, he was a soldier and he did his job. And yeah, he'd jump into a brawl if he felt it was warranted, but this was something else altogether.

Logan grabbed his friend and kept him from hitting the guy again.

"What the hell, man?" Ethan pushed himself to his feet. "I thought we were friends. What the hell?" He wiped the blood from his lip.

Something about the way he said it made Logan think he knew exactly what this was about.

"Guess I just figured you had it coming," Adam said. He stopped straining against Logan's hold and after a second, Logan let him go.

The bartender peeked her head out the door. "Everything all right out here, Adam?" she asked.

"Fine, Vidalia. Go ahead inside."

The guy, Ethan, brushed himself off. "So, is this about Allie? Or Riley?"

Adam lunged forward again, and Logan grabbed his shoulders. Ethan ducked backwards, just out of reach. "I can tell you for a fact, I'm not responsible for Allie's *situation*. I took her out exactly two times and didn't get farther than a g-rated kiss at the door."

"And what about Riley?" Adam asked.

"Not my story to tell. You'll have to take that up with your wife."

"Ex-wife."

Logan hadn't seen the woman approach. He'd been too focused on keeping Adam from decking the stranger again. But he did see the expression on Adam's face change. His anger disappeared, and the tension in his body left, like he'd gone weak.

"What the hell are you doing here, Riley?" he asked, his voice quiet, but kind of quivering underneath.

"One of the benefits of divorce is that I don't have to explain my actions to you anymore," she replied with ice in her voice.

"Not like you ever did," Adam muttered.

The woman—Riley— placed a hand on Ethan's jaw, and looked at the blood dripping from his chin. She was small, slender, pretty, and wearing a high-end suit that didn't really fit the dusty streets of this small Oklahoma town. She had dark brown hair as sleek as a mink, and sparking green eyes that narrowed on Adam. She was at least a foot shorter than him, but didn't look one bit intimidated. "You *hit* him?"

Adam gave her a wry smile. "I don't need to explain myself to you, either."

"I was wrong about you a lot of times, Adam, but I never thought you were a bully. Guess it's a good thing I got out when I did."

Adam's jaw tightened. "Guess so." Without another word, he turned and walked slowly back into the bar. And Logan was pretty sure he wasn't going to get him out of there anytime soon.

Allie stirred the bowl of cookie dough in front of her, longing for a cup of something with a lot of caffeine. The decaf she'd been sipping wasn't doing the trick.

She yawned and pushed the mug away from her in disgust. It had been a long night, followed by a long day. Logan had retreated to the living room after breakfast, and she had tried hard to ignore him, but it wasn't easy.

He had spent most of the morning playing with Jack and Cassie, talking football with her dad and charming her mother with the funnier stories about his time with Adam in Afghanistan.

Her family loved him. He fit right in, and she knew that if any of them found out he was the father of her baby, they'd be browbeating her to marry the man before he changed his mind.

For all she knew, he'd already changed his mind. He hadn't mentioned his ludicrous proposal again.

It had been a relief when Adam suggested they go to the OK Corral to watch football and grab a beer, even though the idea of Adam and Logan and her father spending time together made her nervous. She could only hope that Logan would keep their secret a little bit longer.

She stirred the cookie dough with more force than was necessary, thinking about the infuriating man. She should be happy. She knew that. He had stood up for her with her family. It was sweet in an overbearing kind of way.

But she thought about how he had told her that marriage was her *best option.* She thought about how her family had fawned over him, and she felt the need to use his head for batting practice. The man was frustrating, and what was worse, she found it hard to concentrate on anything else when he was around.

She'd been so focused on Logan that she had somehow volunteered to babysit without even realizing it. Angie and her mom had decided to finish their last-minute Christmas shopping and she'd offered before she could think it over. And to her surprise, her sister agreed.

Allie didn't mind sitting with the kids. She was happy she could help Angie. Her sister hadn't left the kids much at all since Jeff's death, and not ever with Allie. Allie had done her fair share of helping in other ways. She picked Jack up every day after school, and filled Angie's grocery list at least once a week. She cooked meals in the evening. But every time Allie volunteered to watch the kids, Angie had found a reason to say no.

So when Angie finally let her babysit, she couldn't refuse. Her sister had finally decided to trust her. This was major. So she agreed happily, even though she really could have used an afternoon to herself. She had to figure out what she was going to do about Logan wanting to be in the baby's life and wanting to tell her brother the truth.

God, it was a lot.

The television in the next room was playing some animated movie about dragons, and from her spot at the kitchen island, she could see Jack watching from the couch, bouncing with excitement as the dragons took flight. His sister lay next to him, curled up and napping.

Allie finally had a few quiet moments to herself, and as it turned out, the last thing she wanted to think about was Logan Edwards. She wanted to think about Christmas. She grabbed her phone off the counter, clicked through to her favorite Christmas playlist and let holiday classics calm her nerves and fill her with that magical feeling.

She relaxed and sang along while she scooped the cookie dough into balls and placed them on the baking sheet. It was working. She was already feeling a little calmer.

The front door opened and she jumped. Her eyes scanned the living room, thinking first that one of her small wards was escaping. Angie had made a point of telling her what a handful Cassie could be.

She glanced into the living room, but couldn't see the front door from there. Cassie was still asleep, and Jack was now zooming through the room with his arms outstretched, pretending to fly. Then he stopped, and said, "Hey! What's wrong with Uncle Adam?"

That brought Allie into the living room in time to see Logan with Adam's arm around his shoulders, walking him into the den. "He's really sleepy, Jack. Nothing to worry about," Logan said.

They vanished into the den, and in a second, Logan came back out and pulled the door closed behind him.

She sighed and returned to her cookies, but a second later, a tingle on her spine told her that Logan had come into the kitchen.

"Where's Dad?" Allie asked. She could feel the tension creeping back into her body. He was a walking, talking stress trigger and she wondered why she'd ever agreed to let him stay.

"Your dad went home, and I just deposited Adam in his bed."

"Yes, I saw that."

"He ...*might* have had a little too much to drink."

"Because of me? Wouldn't be the first time I've driven one of the Wakeland men to drink."

"Maybe about you at first, but not the last few hours." Logan crossed the room and took a seat at the kitchen island facing Allie.

"Riley?" Allie asked, not really needing the confirmation.

"Yeah. She showed up at the bar. I didn't think she was still around. How'd you know?"

"Riley is the only woman who can make my brother crazier than I can. Is he okay?"

Logan sighed. "I guess. He got wasted and punched the guy she was with. He heard this Ethan character was the last man you were involved with, so..." Logan didn't say more, but Allie felt the need to explain.

"Involved is a strong word. We went out a couple of times. It was before I met you. Anyway, I broke it off after two dates when he cajoled me into a goodnight kiss and then tried to ram his tongue down my throat. Jerk."

"Oh."

"If there had been anything between Ethan and me, or anyone and me, I never would've invited you to my room that night."

His eyes were sharp and discerning and Allie couldn't look at them for long. It felt like he could see too much.

"Your brother punched the guy and it was my fault, Allie. If I had just told him the truth to begin with—"

"Adam has been looking for a reason to punch Ethan Wyatt for years. It has nothing to do with us."

"That's not what it felt like."

"Well, there's a reason. Riley served him with divorce papers the day he got home from a deployment. I was just a kid and I loved Riley, which is probably why no one told me any of this then. But I guess Adam tracked her down. He wanted to talk to her. They'd been through a lot and he wasn't ready to give up. But when he knocked on the door, Ethan answered."

"And you dated the guy?"

"If I had known that, I never would have gone out with him. Angie told me after I dumped him." She thought of the two of them, seeing them in her mind's eye, laughing together, crazy in love. "Riley and Adam were something special. We all thought it would last forever, and I don't think he ever really got over her. He hasn't been serious about a girl since. So him socking Ethan truly *wasn't* about you. Or us."

"That's not the point. It's not right."

"Did you tell him?" Allie asked, dreading his answer.

"Not yet. Adam probably wouldn't remember even if I had." Logan sighed and ran his hands through his short hair. "Your dad's a great guy, Allie, and Adam's my best friend. Every minute I spend with them without saying something feels like a lie."

Relief washed over her. She wasn't ready for them to know. She wasn't ready for the pressure that would put on her. She wasn't ready for the meddling or the number of people who would be giving her their opinions on what she should do.

She needed to figure this out for herself and for her baby before she had everyone else's opinions swirling around in her head. She grabbed the cookie sheet and turned to place it in the oven.

"What stopped you?" she asked.

"I don't know. Your dad said something. About how stress wasn't good for you. About how dangerous it could be. I don't really know anything about pregnant women, but I figured telling them would probably be the most stressful thing I could do to you. And Adam was already so mad, I thought it would only make things worse.

"I want to figure this thing out, Allie. And I'm guessing that once they know, they're gonna want me gone. I can't blame them, but there's a lot we still have to work through, and there's not much time…" He trailed off. "I guess I just didn't want you to have to deal with the fall-out on your own. I've got thirteen days left here. We might as well use them to solve this together."

"Thanks for that."

"I can't keep it from them forever," he said, looking tense. "I know you think it would be better if I took the easy way out, but I can't do that. This is temporary. Just until we come up with a solution we can both live with."

Logan's hands were resting on the kitchen island and Allie placed a hand on top of one of his. Hers immediately tingled from the warmth of his skin. But she ignored that. "You're a good guy, Logan. I know you're trying to do the right thing. But you're not thinking clearly. Let's say we do tell everyone you're the father. Then what?"

"Then I help raise my baby. It's not that complicated." She could see his pulse ticking in his throat, and his fist clenched under her hand. But she needed him to understand why this wouldn't work.

"How many bases have you been stationed at?" Allie asked.

"A few. What's your point?"

"Do you know how often military families move? The average is something like every three years." Allie gentled her tone. "So the best-case scenario is that you'd be really involved with this baby for a few years. He or she would get attached, and then you'd be gone."

He pulled his hand away from hers. "It wouldn't have to be that way." She could see his mind working. Trying to find other options.

"What then? We split the time? Send our baby back and forth across the country? And what about when school starts?" Allie had spent most of the night thinking about this. There was no good option. At least none that she'd come up with.

"Damn it, Allie. Why are we even discussing this? It's not an issue now. When and if it is, we'll figure it out."

"By then it will be too late. I don't want to see my baby hurting the way Jack and Cassie are hurting." Allie pointed toward the living room where Jack sat on the couch, once again engrossed in his TV show.

"It's been over a year, and Jack's still waiting for his daddy to come home. No one can convince him that it's not gonna happen. He goes to bed every night and tells his mom that tomorrow is going to be the day his father comes back. He can't accept it. And that's almost better than the alternative, because once it finally sinks in...once he gives up hope, that little boy is going to be a completely different person."

"So what am I supposed to do, Allie? You want me to walk away like my parents did? To desert my own child and just assume that life will work out for him? I can't do that. I won't. I know better."

His eyes were fiercely determined, and Allie ached for the little boy he'd been. "You know better...because it didn't work out for you. Did it, Logan?"

"No. And my kid isn't going to have to figure it out on his own like I did. I'm gonna be here for him."

"Or her."

"Or her," he said. "People make it work, Allie. We could make it work. If we got married, you could come with me. We could raise our baby together and figure it out as we go."

"That's not a real solution and you know it. I have a life here. My family is here, my work. And you don't want to marry me, not really. It's for the baby, and that's sweet and noble and all that, but it's not enough for me. It's not enough to keep us together if things get tough, and then we'd be right back here trying to figure out what to do all over again. Only this time, our child's heart would be breaking along with our marriage."

"I'm not going to leave my child," Logan said. His voice was sharp, the words, clipped.

Allie sighed. "You won't have a choice. In two weeks, you're gone."

"For three months. But I'll come back. And when I do, I'm going to want to see my baby."

The kitchen timer beeped and broke the intense conversation.

Allie sighed. "It doesn't look like we're going to solve this tonight." She turned to stop the timer. "Can we just keep this between us for now? Just until we've figured out how this is going to work?"

He stared at her. She put a hand on her belly and gazed into his eyes. "Please, Logan. Please keep this secret for me."

Logan held her gaze for a long moment, and she saw his will collapse. "Okay. Okay, fine."

She could see the exhaustion on his face. She knew this was taking a toll on him. Maybe if he had grown up differently, he'd be able to see things her way, but Logan Edwards wasn't anyone else. It would take a lot to convince him that this was the right thing to do. But she'd do it. She'd bring him around for her baby.

She grabbed an oven mitt and pulled the hot cookie tray from the oven.

"I'll give you time, Allie. But I'm not changing my mind."

"Time's all I asked for, Logan. And I'm not changing mine, either."

Logan had retreated to his room after the conversation with Allie, but he couldn't stop thinking about everything she'd said. Maybe she was right. It couldn't be easy for a kid to constantly have to say goodbye to a parent.

Even if they did split time, who would stay with the baby while he was at work? Daycare was fine during the day, but he couldn't very well send his kid back to Allie every time he was in the field or had to pull an overnight duty.

It would be difficult, but it wasn't enough of a reason to keep him from acknowledging his flesh and blood, either.

The house had grown quiet. Eerily quiet, considering there were two small children and an annoyed pregnant woman downstairs.

He was hungry, and the smell of chocolate chip cookies filled the air. He didn't have the answers he needed, but he knew he wasn't going to get any closer to finding them alone in his room.

He opened the door and walked down the short hallway and down the stairs. *Frosty the Snowman* was playing on the television. Allie sat on the couch with Jack snuggled beside her. They were both sound asleep.

Logan glanced at the other side of the couch where Cassie had been tucked in earlier. Her blanket lay discarded on the floor, but the little girl was nowhere in sight. Panic rising, he scanned the room. The door was still shut tight. She couldn't have got outside, could she?

Then there was a *crack* and then a sloshing sound, followed by Cassie's giggles. He followed the sound to the kitchen. The room was mostly cast in shadow, but the refrigerator door was open and the glow from within provided enough light for him to see Cassie sitting on the kitchen floor.

Logan couldn't say exactly how long she'd been awake. He only spent an hour in his room and Allie's oven timer had beeped for the last time twenty minutes ago. But the mess around the child looked like it had taken hours to create.

A dozen eggs were broken in a circle around her. The pantry doors stood open and the bottom third of the shelves had been emptied. Flour, sugar and boxed pasta were dumped around the kitchen. Tiny footprints marked the floor from there to Cassie's current location in front of the fridge. A gallon of milk lay on its side. Most of the bottle was spilled on the floor, but a tiny bit had landed in the plastic cup that Cassie held in front of her. She had a cookie in each hand and was dunking them carefully into her glass.

She looked up at Logan with big blue eyes and a toothy smile. Her blond curls were caked with egg and flour. "Cookie," she said.

The little girl looked so pleased with herself that Logan couldn't help but laugh. Cassie held one of the cookies out to him, trying to get upright at the same time. "Cookie," she said again. And then she slipped on an egg yolk. He reached for her, but missed, and she plopped face first into the flour and sugar pile in front of her.

Her outraged screech split his eardrums.

Logan scooped her up and she quieted, turning a happy grin in his direction. It was almost enough to make him forget about the dripping egg and milk that was soaking through his shirt where he cradled the little girl. Her tiny hand still clutched the cookie, although now it was covered in egg yolk and flour. She tried with all her might to shove it into his mouth. He twisted his face from one side to the other, but the little girl didn't give up. And the cookie smashed into his face four times before it finally crumbled and fell in pieces to the floor.

"What am I going to do with you?" he asked, giving the girl a contemplative look. The obvious solution was a bath, but he'd never given a baby a bath, and he felt weird bathing someone else's kid. He was contemplating his options when Allie hurried into the kitchen and stopped dead in her tracks, staring from the mess in front of her to the little girl in Logan's arms.

"I nodded off for a minute. What happened?"

Cassie looked at Allie and smiled. "Cookie," she said waving the remaining piece of cookie in the air like a trophy.

Allie looked heartbroken, which was an overreaction, in Logan's opinion. "Angie will be home any minute."

"Good. She can help clean up the mess her adorable little sweetheart created."

"You don't understand. This is the first time she's left the kids with me since Jeff…. It's the first time she's left Cassie with me at all. She'll never trust me with them again."

Logan glanced at the destruction in the kitchen and thought that might not be such a bad thing, but he had the good sense to keep his opinion to himself. He didn't know why it was so important to Allie, but it obviously was.

"Okay, you take care of her," he said shoving the batter-covered child into Allie's arms. "I'll do something with this." He gestured towards the disaster area that had been a kitchen a short time ago.

"You don't have to do that."

"No time to argue. Just trust me. It'll all be okay."

Allie looked reluctant, but she nodded and hurried down the hall to the first-floor bathroom. Logan spent the next thirty minutes scrubbing every washable surface in the kitchen. He was just dumping the last bucket of water down the sink when Angie and Beth walked through the front door.

The strain and tension that had weighed down Angie's face had eased a little, and Logan wondered if the day out had done her some good.

"What happened here?" she asked as she walked toward the kitchen. She took in the empty bucket, the mop, the sponges and cleaning supplies and then she narrowed her eyes suspiciously at Logan.

He shrugged. "Just thought I'd help clean up a little since Allie was busy with the kids."

"Uh-huh. And where are my children and my darling sister?"

Allie came out of the bathroom right on cue. She held the freshly bathed little girl in her arms.

"I thought I heard you," Allie said. "Did you two have fun?"

"It was very productive," her mother said. "I think Christmas is going to be a good one for the kids this year. I hope we weren't gone too long, dear. You look tired."

"Not at all." Allie turned to her sister. "It's good for you to get out once in a while, Angie." Allie kissed Cassie's forehead and handed the little girl back to her mother. "Jack's sleeping on the couch."

"How were my little monkeys?" Angie asked, rubbing noses with Cassie, who giggled.

"They were angels," Allie said in a very convincing tone. Logan would have been convinced, too, if he hadn't spent the last thirty minutes cleaning up after Hurricane Cassie.

"Really?" There was doubt in her voice.

"Of course," Allie said.

"Then why is your houseguest covered in flour and chocolate?" All eyes turned to Logan. He glanced down at his jeans, which were still caked in egg. Puffs of flour clung to his shirt and he was pretty sure his face was still streaked with chocolate from the cookie Cassie had force-fed him.

"Cookie," Cassie said.

"I'm a messy baker." Logan rubbed a chocolate streak from his chin, with his thumb.

"Angels, huh?" Angie asked, raising an eyebrow in her sister's direction.

"Complete angels," Allie replied. "Aren't they always?"

CHAPTER SEVEN

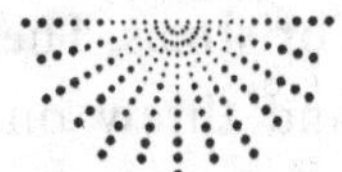

4 DAYS BEFORE CHRISTMAS

*A*llie woke up sore and exhausted. She had collapsed after the children left the night before. Her back hurt from bending over the tub and washing her niece. Muscles in every part of her body ached, and she could only imagine how much worse it would have been if she'd had to crawl around on her hands and knees cleaning up the mess Cassie had made in the kitchen. It was hard to admit, but Logan had been a huge help.

That should have made her happy, but it didn't. As a matter of fact, it made her even more annoyed.

Yesterday had been a test. Not just of her babysitting skills, but of her ability to handle a child of her own. As much as Allie insisted that she was prepared to be a single mother, the truth was she had no idea if she was up for the challenge. Yesterday had been a trial run and she'd failed miserably.

She threw her legs over the side of the bed and heaved herself into a standing position. Her feet hurt immediately. She tried to look down at her swollen toes, but couldn't see past her belly.

She had one job to do: convince Logan that she could raise a child on her own and didn't need his help. Yesterday had proven the exact opposite.

She stomped over to her dresser and pulled out one of the few remaining outfits that fit around her ever-growing form. She needed to put herself in a better mood. After all, there were only four days until Christmas and she wasn't about to waste them being angry and hiding in her room.

Only four days until Christmas. They needed a tree!

She took a shower and threw on her stretchy maternity pants and an oversized sweater, spent a few minutes on her hair and makeup and told herself it wasn't because of Logan. Not that it really mattered what her face looked like. She didn't think she was likely to attract any man right now, and that was fine by her.

It was still early, but sunlight was peeking in the windows by the time Allie crept into the kitchen.

She grabbed her keys off the hook by the door and pulled her coat from the closet. She was just slipping it over her arms when she heard footsteps on the stairs.

"Sneaking out?" Logan asked. His voice was as warm and rich as the chocolate chip cookies she'd baked the night before.

"I'm not sneaking. This is my house, and I'm an adult. I come and go as I please."

He held up both hands. "I'm sorry. I don't know what I did, but I'm sorry."

She narrowed her eyes on him and tried to give him the same withering stare she'd seen her mother use so many times throughout her childhood. "You're here. You're here and you're ruining my Christmas spirit. I'm trying to be jolly, dammit."

Logan smiled. Part of her wanted to slap the smile off his face and another part of her got all excited when he flashed that ridiculous dimple.

"Well, in the spirit of Christmas, I think we should make

peace. We need to be able to talk to each other civilly if we're ever going to get through this."

She shrugged. "I can be civil."

"I was hoping my charm would win you over," he said with a grin.

"Without the benefit of alcohol and the threat of a bar fight, you probably wouldn't have seemed that charming in the first place," she lied.

He shrugged. "Then it's a shame you can't drink, because *with* alcohol, I'm a regular Sir Lancelot."

Allie smiled a little. She was okay with making peace, but she still wanted to get out of the house as soon as possible. A little alone time before the family descended.

"So since we're now acquaintances who can speak politely, can I ask where you're going?"

"It's Christmas tree day," she said. "Or it will be, as soon as I text the family and tell them it is. And before we can load up and head over to Holiday Ranch, I have to pick up pastries from Sunny's Place." And maybe linger over coffee and a donut and some solitude.

"You need snacks to put up a Christmas tree?"

"No. You need snacks to keep the kids entertained and the grown-ups warm while we walk around in search of the *perfect* tree. Usually it'd be done by now, but we wanted to wait for Adam to come home. It's kind of a family tradition."

Logan didn't look like he was understanding, but Allie didn't have time to explain. She turned to grab her shoes.

"Wait. I have questions."

She turned back to face him and saw the wonder in his eyes. It was almost endearing.

"Shoot," she said, perching on a stool to pull the shoes onto her feet.

"First, I'm wondering about the tree. Isn't that a lot of work considering it will only be up for a few days?"

"It's not work. It's fun! And it wouldn't be Christmas without a tree. Mmm, especially a real tree, so you can smell the pine. There's something about searching the lot and finding the right tree. It's different every year, but always seems perfect."

"And the whole family goes?"

"Yeah. We usually go the day after Thanksgiving, but like I said, we waited for Adam." She saw the look on his face, and without being told, she knew that he'd never experienced anything like what she described. "Haven't you ever had a real Christmas tree before?"

"A couple of the foster homes I was in had fake trees, but I spent most of my time at group homes and Christmas was like any other day." He didn't say it with sadness in his voice. It was matter-of-fact, which made Allie feel even worse. She tried to imagine what it would be like to have no family. No happy memories. No childhood holidays to look back on.

Allie couldn't imagine growing up like that. She'd believed in Santa Claus far longer than most of the kids her age. Christmas had always been full of magic for her. She couldn't imagine it any other way.

"Then you have to come with us."

Logan's eyes widened. "I do?"

"You do. And I'm not taking no for an answer."

"I don't know. It's a family thing. Shouldn't it just be family?"

You are family, something inside her said. Maybe it was the baby's voice. She didn't say it aloud. "The more, the merrier. Besides, we're going to be getting three trees. We need all the strong backs we can get."

Logan smiled and Allie tried to ignore the slight swell of her heart. "Any more questions?"

"Tons."

Allie rolled her eyes. "Then you better grab some shoes. You can ask me on the way to Sunny's."

He glanced toward the den. "Should we wake Adam?"

"Not for the pre-game," she said. "I'll text him at kickoff."

~

They'd lingered over breakfast together at the Big Falls diner, and Allie made calls and sent texts, and set everything up. Then they walked along Main Street, where every lamppost bore a wreath, and every shop window was decked for the holiday. They headed to the only place with a pink and white striped awning, instead of a green and white striped awning, Sunny's Place, where they picked up dozens of cookies and pastries. Sunny had filled their two-gallon Thermos jug with hot cocoa, too.

And later, with the family all behind them, ready for action, they drove beneath an arching HOLIDAY RANCH sign, and parked beside the smaller of two barns.

Allie's parents pulled in right behind them in David's shiny red pickup truck. And Angie and her brood brought up the rear in her SUV.

Adam had ridden with David and Beth. He was quiet and looked as if he was still suffering the effects of the booze he'd had the night before.

"It doesn't look like they're open," Logan said, looking at the all-but-deserted place. There were no trees in sight and he wondered if Allie had come to the wrong address.

"Just trust me," Allie said, pulling into a parking spot and opening the car door. It was still early and there weren't any other cars around, although Logan did see ample room for parking beside the small barn.

They had barely taken a step when a pretty strawberry blonde stepped out of the little barn pulling her jacket around her shoulders and greeting Allie with a hug. "I see you're still pregnant," she asked with a smile.

"Yeah, yeah rub it in," Allie replied, then to Logan, "She had hers a month ago."

"Three and a half weeks," she corrected.

"It's a helluva story. Remind me to tell you later."

"Glad to be the source of amusement," Kiley said.

"How's the baby?"

"Diana is great. She's with her auntie in the house. "I hear your big brother's home and that he brought a friend. Is this him?" This with a look at Logan.

"Kiley Kellogg McIntyre, meet Logan Edwards. He's in Adam's unit and came home to spend the holidays with us."

He took her hand, gave it a polite squeeze. "It's a real pleasure," he said.

"Thank you for your service."

He always felt odd when people said that, and glanced Allie's way to distract himself from having to answer. Her eyes sparkled in the morning light. Her cheeks were pink and her smile beamed as she spoke to the other woman. Logan had always heard people say pregnant women glowed, but he'd never noticed it. But as he looked at Allie, he saw it. She was shining like the sun.

The rest of her family had arrived.

"Can I talk you into taking one of the pre-cut trees?" Kiley asked. "You don't need to worry about it lasting. We've only got a few days to go, and I guarantee they're fresh cut. Otherwise, you have your work cut out for you." She added, for Logan's benefit, "We bought the Christmas Tree farm that borders our place," she said. "Owners retired to Sedona. But it's *way* up back."

Allie said, "I've been going *way up back* since I was a kid," Allie said. "This year is no different."

"Allie, are you sure?" her mother asked. "It's quite a hike and you're hardly in the condition to make it."

"Not to mention you're past your due date," Logan said.

She rolled her eyes. "A walk will do me good. Maybe it'll convince this baby to stop being so stubborn and make an appearance."

Kiley shook her head. "Not on my watch. You wait right here. I'll have Rob hook up the wagon. You can do a horse-drawn hay ride up to the pine lot. Go on into the shop. I'll be right back."

She hurried away before Allie could argue.

"All right everyone, you heard Kiley. While we wait, let's pick out an ornament!" Beth's voice carried over the chatter and all the Wakelands quieted down and made their way into the small barn.

"You coming?" Allie asked when Logan lagged behind.

"I'm not sure. What are we doing now?"

"Every year, we each pick out a special ornament that means something to us, to remind us of the year gone by. Kiley has a gift shop here. She has all kinds of ornaments. So...we might as well get them here."

Logan held back, thinking about that. The only thing special about the past year, was meeting Allie, and making a baby with her.

The rest of the group had already gone in through the big rolling door and Logan was happy he had Allie all to himself for another few minutes.

"Tell me about the one you picked out last year."

"Last year was different." The smile had fled her face all of the sudden.

He knew that. Stupid to bring it up and dampen her joy.

Yesterday he'd been so annoyed with her, he wished he never had to speak to her again, but today in the glow of the early morning sunlight, she looked sweet and tempting and he found himself having a hard time keeping his hands off her.

"What will you get this year?" he asked, to bring her smile back. "One with a baby on it?"

Allie tucked a strand of hair behind her ear. "Maybe."

"Any suggestions for someone like me?"

"You can't think of anything you've done this year that you want to remember?"

Logan flashed his most charming smile. "Nothing that I think will be found on an ornament."

Allie's face flushed, and she couldn't hide her smile. "Maybe start with something easy. Like a snowman with your name on it."

~

They took the wagon ride through the woods and up a hill. Everyone laughed and talked, and the kids played and bickered and giggled. Beth hugged her husband's arm to her side and leaned her head on his shoulder and gazed at the boisterous crew of their offspring in a kind of rapture. Angie's forced smile was convincing enough to fool her kids, but no one else, and Adam just looked lonely.

They'd disembarked, and split up at the beginning of this scavenger hunt. Allie's parents had gone in one direction and he'd glimpsed them smooching behind a needled bough once. Adam had gone with Angie and the kids so he could carry Cassie on his shoulders.

Logan was following Allie through what seemed to be an endless forest.

"How about this one?" Logan asked, pointing at a tree that looked exactly as green and perfect as every other tree on the lot.

Allie pursed her lips looking the tree up and down and then she moved around it in a circle. "Nope. It has a bare spot."

"I'm beginning to understand why Kiley's husband brought a book along to read while he waited on the wagon. What was it? *War and Peace?*"

"Nothing wrong with being picky."

"As picky as you are, I'd think you would have bought a fake tree years ago. Could save yourself an awful lot of time."

Her nose crinkled in disgust. "Not if I live to be one hundred and ten. I'll still drag my wrinkly, old butt up this hill and come back down with a real tree."

"I bet you will. So tell me, what is it about this back lot that's so special?" Logan asked, wanting to know more about the woman next to him.

"My parents got their first Christmas tree from these same woods, the year they got married. After that, it became a tradition." Her cheeks flushed a little. "It's corny and silly, but I love it."

"I think that's sweet." He imagined their child. A little girl with Allie's dark brown curls, running at her mother's side. Or a little boy with her mischievous gleam in his eyes. In Logan's imagination, he was there, too. Walking right beside them, and he wished that could be reality, but maybe Allie was right. Maybe the only thing he could guarantee his child was a broken heart when he had to leave.

"How about that one?" he asked pointing to another generic looking pine.

"Too short," she said walking further down the row of evergreens.

He cast his eyes around for a taller one and found it two rows over. "How about that one?" He pointed.

"That one...*might* work." Allie hurried toward it, and circled the tree a few times. "Nope...see the brown needles on the back side? They'll be falling off before we even get it in the door."

They were nearly to the back corner of the lot. "Allie, I know you always get your trees from this area, but maybe we should just get one of the pre-cut ones. They looked nice. You know, no brown spots."

"No, it's here. I know it is."

"We're almost out of trees," Logan tried to point out logically, but Allie wasn't listening.

Then suddenly she shouted, scaring him half out of his shoes, "That's it, Logan! Do you see it?" She pointed to the last tree in the corner of the field. It was a beautiful tree, but so were the other two thousand they'd passed to find it.

"What makes this one the right tree?" he asked, watching Allie admire the tree as they went to take a closer look.

"It just is! This is the *perfect* tree."

When he saw the way her face lit as she gazed at the conifer, Logan had to agree.

"I guess I'm lucky you weren't this picky the night we met."

She crooked an eyebrow at him. "You never would have passed the test."

He smiled. "But the tree does?"

"Yes, this is the one!" She was so excited she practically bounced, which he imagined was no easy task for a pregnant woman.

"Great." He crouched on the cold ground with the hand saw Rob McIntyre had provided and got to work.

"Be careful. Make sure you hold the saw level or it'll never stand up straight in the tree stand," Allie said.

He had to lie on his side to saw all the way through. Allie stood over him, holding the center of the tree to keep it from pinching the saw blade. He made the final cut and the tree tumbled from her grip falling to the ground. He couldn't stop himself from smiling at the sound of her delighted laughter.

Then he said, "You had to pick the furthest tree from the wagon."

"Not by a long shot," she said, pointing up ahead. "There are three more lots that way. Next time I should make you go through all of them."

"Next time, Mr. McIntyre better bring his entire library."

They realized at the same time that next time, Logan might

not be there and they both fell silent. Logan pulled the tree to the path and as soon as he spotted them, Rob McIntyre hopped down from the wagon to help load it up.

"That's a beauty," he said.

Logan glanced around. "Where's the rest of the crew?"

"Oh, they won't be back for a while yet. Finding the perfect tree takes time," Allie explained.

McIntyre said, "I'll hike out and check on them. You two go ahead and settle into the wagon. You should get off your feet, Allie. I put your snacks under the seat."

Logan helped Allie climb onto the wagon and scrambled up after her. She sat down on the hard, wooden bench, then tracked down the thermos full of cocoa and started to pour it into a pair of the foam cups they'd brought.

"You really do this every year?" he asked, eager to hear more about her childhood.

"Every except last. Like I said, last year was different. Angie got the news about Jeff two days after Thanksgiving."

Logan swallowed the lump in his throat. You couldn't be in his line of work and not be aware of what could happen, but he'd never seen someone who was going through the loss first hand. It wouldn't be like that if it happened to him. He was a loner. No connections. No ties.

At least not until now.

"That must've been awful."

"Angie was a mess. Living on the base in Fort Sill with the kids. No family down there. So I went down to get her, but she insisted on having Christmas there, in the last place where they'd been a family together. I tried to help with the kids and the arrangements. But I couldn't help with her broken heart."

Allie shivered and Logan knew it had nothing to do with the chill of the morning. Still he put his arm around her shoulders and felt her relax into him just a little.

"I was trying to hold it together for the kids. And Angie was doing everything the way she and Jeff always had, but that only made it harder on Jack. Cassie was too little to know what was going on, but poor Jack. He was sure Santa was going to bring his daddy home." A tear spilled onto her cheek.

"We woke up on Christmas morning and Jack ran into the living room, yelling for his dad. When he didn't find him, he lost it. It just broke him. He was so disappointed."

An ache settled into Logan's chest, imagining what little Jack had gone through. "What'd you do?"

"The only thing I could think of. I threw everything in my car. The presents, the kids, Angie, and I drove them to my house. I called Adam on the way and told him what had happened. I told him and our parents to meet us at my house and bring food.

"It took us hours to get home, but the whole way I was thinking, what am I going to do when we get there? How am I going to fix this? Then we pulled into the driveway and about five minutes later Adam arrived with more presents for the kids. And then…then it just got amazing."

"How so?" He was watching the emotions cross her face as she spoke, feeling every one of them with her.

"The locals must have spread the word, because all day neighbors stopped in with food and gifts. A roast turkey from Rosie over at the Big Falls diner. Pies and Christmas cookies from Sunny's. Toys for the kids. Dolls and books and videogames. I don't know how they did it on such short notice. On Christmas Day of all things. It was like magic. The whole town coming together to bring Christmas to these two kids who'd lost their dad." The tears were streaming down Allie's face now and Logan knew if he was the crying type, he'd have shed a few, too.

His heart ached for Jack, and he made a mental note to grab a couple of things for Angie's kids before Christmas morning.

"That's incredible. It makes me wish I'd grown up in a town like this.

"It's not perfect. We have a humbug here and there. You'd fit right in."

"I bet you charm the socks off every single one of them."

"Not *every* one. There's Mr. Andrews. He is definitely not a fan of mine." Allie said, smiling.

The sunlight shone on her dark hair and made it look lighter, like there were swirls of gold in it, and he longed to reach out his fingers and feel the silky softness for himself. He resisted the urge.

"That's enough to declare him the town grouch? What did you do to poor Mr. Andrews? You didn't throw him into the middle of a bar fight, did you?"

"I stole his dog." Allie looked quite pleased with herself.

"I might have heard part of this story. But I'm dying to hear your version."

"It happened one spring. I was driving home when a huge storm hit. The rain was coming in sideways and the wind was howling. The sky was pitch black. I had just turned onto my parents' street when I heard the tornado warnings on the radio and the siren started going off. Anyway, I drove past Mr. Andrews' house, and there was his poor dog, Rusty, chained to a post in the middle of the yard with nothing to protect him from the weather." Allie shrugged, like that explained everything.

"Keep going. You just got to the good part."

"That's it, really. I stopped the car, unhooked the dog and took him home."

"In the middle of a tornado warning, you stopped to steal your neighbor's dog." Logan looked at her, incredulous.

"Well, when you say it like that, it sounds crazy. But I couldn't let the poor thing suffer out there. He was the sweetest dog. A big shaggy mutt with more fur than brains. I took him home, and he wreaked havoc on Mom's furniture for a while and ate everything in sight, but I was crazy about that dog. I never told anyone in the family where he came from. I would have kept him, but Mr. Andrews saw the whole thing. A few days later, Jimmy Corona was at my door."

"Jimmy Co—"

"Big Falls police chief. He said I had to give the dog back and apologize or Andrews would press charges. He said if I let him take the dog, he wouldn't tell my folks. So I didn't have much choice. But I told him to tell Andrews that if I saw him mistreat that poor animal again, he'd lose more than just his dog."

Logan was grinning like an idiot by the end of the story. "You told the police chief that." She nodded. Her version of the tale was much more entertaining than Adam's had been, and it cast her in an entirely different light. She wasn't the family screw-up her brother believed her to be. She was a strong, stubborn woman who knew exactly what she wanted and did everything she could to get it. He liked that. He liked her. More and more, with every minute he spent with her. And he had no idea what he was going to do about it.

"So, tell me about you," she said. "You really don't know anything about your family?"

"I know enough. They gave me up two hours after I was born. There were health issues, most of them due to my mother taking drugs throughout her pregnancy. Luckily, I escaped without any permanent damage. But it was enough to keep interested adoptive parents away. When I was eight, I received a clean bill of health, but by that time, I was well past the ideal adoption age. So, I bounced around the system until I was a teenager, and when I couldn't stand it anymore, I ran away. I figured being on my own was better than being in a group home. As soon as I was old enough, I got my GED and enlisted."

He wasn't bitter or angry about his past. He didn't tell her so she'd feel sorry for him. He just wanted her to understand why he couldn't desert their baby. Even if she wanted him to. Even if she believed in her stubborn way that it was the only way things could work. He couldn't do it. Not ever.

"Did you ever try to find your parents?" she asked. Her eyes held the pity and sorrow he always saw when he told people about his family. He hated that look. And he hated seeing it on Allie's face even more. He didn't need pity. He'd had made a life for himself without his parents. Without anyone.

"No."

"Aren't you curious about them? About why they gave you up?"

"I know everything I need to know. They didn't even wait around to see if I was going to make it before they signed me over to the state. When I was little, when I needed them, I spent years imagining them coming back for me. They never did. I wasted enough time and energy on that. I don't need them anymore. Probably never did."

He couldn't expect her to understand. She came from a home full of love. A town that transformed into a fairy tale when bad things happened. She'd told him once that her hometown was magic. She was magic, too, he thought.

He looked into her sparkling eyes and then he kissed her. He just cupped her face with a palm and he leaned in and kissed her, long, and slow and deep.

"Uncle Adam says if I'm real quiet, maybe we'll see a deer or a rabbit or something," Jack yelled at the top of his lungs, as he came charging out of the tree lot at a dead run.

They pulled apart. Allie's brown eyes were wide and full of questions.

Angie followed with the toddler on her hip and Adam brought up the rear, looking like he'd just been hit by a steam roller. "I'd tell him he might see bigfoot if it would make him keep his voice down," Adam muttered dragging a massive pine tree behind him. Rob McIntyre was close behind, and helped him load it. "I adore that kid, but I'm seriously thinking about getting him a muzzle for Christmas."

Angie gave her brother a sharp elbow to the ribs and tried to hide a smile. "It's not Jack's fault you can't hold your booze," she retorted.

"Nope. It's Dad's fault. Bad genes."

"Your father's genes are excellent. Don't go blaming us for your shortcomings," Beth said from the other side of the tree line. Logan wasn't sure how she'd gotten close enough to hear without her children noticing, but she didn't look like she was about to tolerate them taking jabs at her husband.

David whispered something in his wife's ear and Logan saw her cheeks turn pink. He wondered what that was like. Having a relationship like that. A love like that. He was still wondering about it when the wagon pulled back into the parking lot and slowed to a stop. His eyes were drawn to Allie and he let himself imagine for just a second.

CHAPTER EIGHT

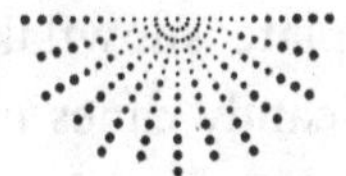

Logan felt like he'd been transported into a Hallmark Channel Christmas movie. Allie's family decorated a pine tree in her living room as if it was the most important task on the planet. Nothing about the world around him seemed real. Even the handful of things that he'd thought he understood, things about family were completely different than what he'd thought.

He'd pictured people, and a nice home, and meals at a table, and parents who attended school functions. But he'd never ever once imagined the love of the thing. It was like a big, glowing, sphere that emanated from each of them and encompassed all of them.

And somehow or other, it encompassed him, too.

He looked at his best friend, who stood there arranging silver tinsel, one delicate strand at a time. A month ago, tough-as-nails Captain Adam Wakeland had been riding beside him in a Humvee over rutted dirt roads in Afghanistan.

His gaze wandered back to Allie. It didn't stay very long on anything or anyone else. She held a decoration in her hand, a tiny gold frame in the shape of a house with a picture of her family inside. The photo showed grade-school versions of Allie, Angie and Adam with their parents, younger than they were now but every bit as much in love. It glowed from their eyes and gleamed in their smiles.

Logan had always thought of Christmas ornaments as just colorful balls in red and green, but the ornaments in this house were different. Most of them were the kinds of things kids make in school. Paper plate snowflakes, clothespin reindeer, popsicle-stick sleds, and candy canes made from red and white pipe cleaners all twisted together. Logan had made them as a kid too, but no one had been around to wrap his hand-made creations in tissue paper and save them for Christmases to come. He'd rarely even had a tree to hang them on, and usually left them in the classroom.

Mixed in with the school projects were special ornaments that Allie's parents had bought for each of their children every year. They'd kept some of them, and divided the rest between Allie and Angie, who traded them back and forth each year. Adam would join in that tradition once he was home long enough to have a Christmas tree of his own to decorate. Allie explained all that.

Because her family couldn't stand the idea of Allie decorating her tree alone, they always joined her to put it up and add ornaments before taking their own trees home.

They recited memories as they hung each ornament. A tiny pink cradle from the year Allie was born. A pair of ballet shoes to honor her first dance recital. A baseball bat for the time Adam's team had won the regionals. There were dozens of memories hanging from the tree in short order, a visual time-line of their family history.

It made Logan wonder about his own parents. He wondered if they'd had other kids—which would mean he might have siblings. He used to obsess about that, always checking the faces of every kid he met to decide if they looked like him.

He'd got over that habit with a lot of effort. It had been years since he'd given his birth family a second thought. But being in this house was bringing it all back.

Late afternoon sun shone through the window and glinted off Allie's dark locks as she paced around the tree, making sure every detail was just right. Logan couldn't help but smile. Their child would know this kind of love, he realized, and knowing that made him overwhelmingly happy, but he also felt a little out of place. He was the one thing that didn't fit into this happy little picture. He was the Grinch, and they were the Whos.

Adam finished with his tinsel on the tree and sat down on the couch across from Logan.

"So, Edwards, got any plans for this evening?"

In Logan's experience, Adam only grinned like that when he was about to ask someone to do something they weren't going to like. But here in bizzaro-Christmas world, maybe things were different.

"That depends. Why do you ask?"

Adam's grin grew bigger. "I want to take you out to dinner. You're my friend. You're spending the holidays with us. I just want to do something nice."

If it wasn't for the over-the-top smile, Logan might have believed him.

"Don't buy it," Allie interrupted. "He's up to something." She had returned to the box of ornaments on the coffee table and was now pulling colorful knit Christmas stockings out of the box. Each one had a name embroidered across the top. Adam. Allie. Angie. "From when we were kids," she told Logan. "I don't put anything in them, I just like hanging them every year."

"Stop changing the subject." Adam picked up a pillow and tossed it at his sister. It bounced off her face and landed in the ornament box and she shot her brother a dirty look. He grinned at her. "I scored tickets to the biggest holiday event our neighbor town of Tucker Lake has to offer, and I want to take you with me."

"And what is this event?" Logan asked suspiciously.

"The Haggerty House Holiday Hootenanny."

"I'm sure I didn't hear you correctly. A Hootenanny? What self-respecting business throws a hootenanny?"

"It's more like a country style holiday ball," Allie said. "But hootenanny adds a dose of downhome charm, don't you think?"

"Not to mention the alliteration factor," Logan shot back, and they shared a smile that lasted a beat too long. He felt Adam's frown without even seeing it and quickly dragged his eyes off his C.O.'s sister. "So, why are we attending a ball?"

"I was invited by a high school friend, but she doesn't want to leave her sister home alone, so you're my wingman."

Logan rolled his eyes. A blind date. Adam was trying to set him up on a blind date. And Allie was standing right there, her little body straining to hold his baby inside. "That sounds like a great time, Adam, but I'm...uh...busy." Lame.

"Doing what?"

Logan tried to think of anything he might be busy doing, but since he was staying at Allie's house and didn't even have his own car with him, he was having a hard time coming up with any excuse that sounded believable.

"Who's the friend?" Allie asked, her tone suddenly irritated and sharp.

"Sidney Thompson. Her sister graduated with you. She's a pretty girl, Logan. I swear. Tell him, Allie."

"Sure, she's pretty. Also, has all the depth of a teaspoon and the personality of a wet dishrag, but pretty is all that counts."

Adam gaped at her. "What are *you* so worked up about? I'm not asking *you* to go out with her."

"I wouldn't want to go anyway. I have decorating to do. The wind knocked down some of my lights and I refuse to let Christmas come without fixing them."

Logan smiled to himself. The house was already decorated with so many lights, he'd done a double take the first time he'd seen it after dark. It must have taken weeks to put them all up and he hoped to goodness she hadn't done it all herself.

But the thing that truly put the smile on his face was the tone in Allie's voice. She sounded jealous of this Sidney's sister, and that had him grinning like an idiot.

"I'd really prefer to stay in anyway," he said to Adam, but his gaze couldn't seem to stay off Allie. "Gotta catch up on my sleep. Plus, one of us needs to stay with Allie. She's past her due date."

"Since when are you Sir Galahad?" Adam asked. He looked from Logan to Allie and back again. "Anyway, it's not an issue. I got a ticket for Lexie, too. We're all going." Allie rolled her eyes and Adam went on. "And, I didn't want to mention this before, Logan, but you need to get back out there."

"Oh, *does* he." It wasn't a question. Allie's voice had dropped an octave. She sounded really pissed off.

Logan sent Adam a withering glare. "Shut up, Adam."

"No, don't shut up, Adam. You know I can't resist juicy gossip. Is our guest trying to get past some big break-up?" The edge in her voice could slice a ripe tomato.

"It's nothing," Logan said flatly.

"Oh, come on, Edwards, we don't have secrets around here." Adam elbowed him and grinned. "He met some girl before we deployed, and he's been hung up on her ever since. Casanova here didn't even catch her full name. What was it again? Sally?"

It was Allie. "I never said."

"Well, whatever it was, he woke up and she was gone." He clapped Logan's shoulder. "It's a lost cause, buddy. You gotta let it go."

Logan couldn't remember the last time he'd blushed, but his face sure felt hot right then. He tried to avoid looking at Allie, but his eyes caught the hint of a smile on her face.

"As for you," Adam said turning to his sister, "I've missed you like crazy, and I want you to come with us. Besides, your house's halls are decked to the rafters, and anything else you need done, I'll do it for you myself, tomorrow. Edwards'll help, right pal?" He slapped Logan's shoulder again. "We're going to Haggerty House at seven and you're both coming."

∼

If it was possible to kill someone with a single look, Katy Thompson would have been on the coroner's table before they'd finished their appetizers. Allie sat at a round table at Haggerty House in Tucker Lake, beneath mistletoe and party lights and literal boughs of holly. To her left was Logan, and to his left, Katy. To her right, Adam, then his vapid date Sidney.

Allie had disliked Katy and Sidney Thompson all through high school. She'd tried not to, but it was impossible. They were those kinds of girls who downplayed their intelligence because they thought it made them more attractive to boys. Most girls got over that mindset by the time high school was over, but apparently not these two. Katy played the bimbo card with every sentence she uttered. After five minutes, Allie was ready to vomit and after ten, she wanted to stab the other woman in the eye with a fork.

Haggerty House was packed. Allie scanned the large cream-colored room and saw a few familiar faces—a lot of Big Falls folks made the Hootenanny a holiday tradition, including Darryl Champlain, the songwriter, and his wife, her doctor, known to one and all as Doc Sophie. Bobby Joe and Vidalia Brand McIntyre were there, too, dancing up a storm. The place was filled to capacity. She was glad. The Haggerty girls, who ran the place with their grandmother, had been through a lot and she was happy to see them doing so well.

"Allie, you're so lucky that you don't have to worry about what you eat anymore," Katy said, pulling Allie's attention back to the table. The five of them had just returned from the buffets, which were loaded with food. Ham, turkey, roast beef, potatoes and gravy and every imaginable side. There were several other tables holding multi-tiered pyramids of mouthwatering desserts.

Allie had filled her plate until it wouldn't hold any more and she was seriously considering going back for more. She restrained herself only after looking at the dessert tables and knowing she wanted to save room for that.

Katy and Sidney had made themselves salads with fat free dressing on the side. It looked about as appetizing as a patch of Red River crabgrass. Allie would have said so too, if she didn't have mashed potatoes in her mouth. But Katy didn't wait for a response. "Of course, I've always been naturally thin, but you can never be too careful."

Allie swallowed her potatoes, dabbed her mouth with a red linen napkin, and muttered, "Probably the only *natural* thing about you," behind it.

Logan heard her and choked on a bite of buttery homemade bread, but no one else at the table heard.

"So when are you due, Allie?" Katy continued, oblivious.

"Day before yesterday. But the doctor said first pregnancies often go past the due date." She answered as nicely as she could, feeling a little bad for being so bitchy.

But then the twit said, "Are you sure it's not twins?" And she put a hand on Logan's arm and leaned closer. "She's so big!"

"I was gonna ask the same thing," Sidney said with a saccharine smile.

Allie's fingers tightened around the handle of her knife.

Logan cleared his throat and shifted his chair a little closer to Allie's. "So Katy, tell me about yourself," he said.

Katy turned her attention to Logan, and Allie tried to ignore them. She hated that he was paying attention to the wench, but she supposed she should be glad it had happened before she'd committed a capital offense.

She took a few bites of her dinner and tried to engage in conversation with Adam instead. It took less than a minute for her to realize that Sidney was determined to monopolize all of his attention. She definitely wasn't going to find any scintillating conversation at this table.

This had been a bad idea. Allie shoveled in another bite of her dinner and was immediately full. This late in the pregnancy her appetite was huge, but the baby left very little room for her stomach to expand, so she always seemed to take way more than she could eat. She looked around the table. The others were barely touching their food. She couldn't stand being trapped as the fifth wheel on a double date for much longer.

Katy whispered something into Logan's ear. Allie wished she could have a drink. If she could have a glass of Grandma Haggerty's famous spiced rum punch, she might be able to get through this night with a smile on her face.

Katy was eyeing Logan the way Allie had eyed the dessert bar a few minutes ago. *Nope, probably not.*

She pushed her plate away and was contemplating how difficult it would be to fake contractions when Logan spoke up.

"Allie, are you ready to show me the Christmas tree?"

"What?"

"The Haggerty House Holiday Tree. You mentioned it this morning. How it's the biggest tree in Tucker Lake. I've been dying to get a closer look."

Katy placed a hand on Logan's arm. "I could show you," she offered, batting long fake eyelashes at him.

"Not a chance. You're still eating. I'm sure Allie doesn't mind. Do you, Allie?"

She tried not to look too smug, but she couldn't wipe the smile off her face. "Of course not." She stood up, bumping her giant belly on the table and shaking the water glasses in the process, but not even that could detract from the satisfaction of seeing the look on Katy's face.

Logan placed a hand on her elbow and together they walked toward the large open staircase.

"Thanks for helping me escape," Logan whispered once they were out of earshot.

"*You?* I thought I was the one desperate to get out of there. I had forgotten exactly how annoying Katy Thompson could be."

"Not sure how you could ever forget that. I'm pretty sure I never will."

"So you weren't falling for the brainless beauty routine?"

"I like women with a little more…substance."

"Was that a fat joke? 'Cause I can send you right back there."

"Please don't. I can't stand another minute of listening to her talk about her fitness routine, and I honestly think that might be the most interesting thing about her." He smiled down at her, and a warm feeling spread through her chest.

"Adam will be so disappointed that his match-making plans failed," Allie said, picking up speed as the tree came into view.

"*I'm* disappointed. I thought Adam liked me more than that."

Allie stopped beside the staircase. The center of the dining room was open all the way up, with the second-floor dining, loft style. A huge Christmas tree reached clear up to the rafters. It was covered in twinkling white lights, red velvet ribbons, and silver and gold ornaments. Allie had photographed it three years ago and the Haggerty sisters had liked the shot so much they'd ordered postcards with the image on the front. It was the first photograph she'd taken that had made money, and it had set her on the path to figuring out what she wanted to do with her life.

She gazed at that tree and felt holiday magic wrap its soothing glitter around her aching soul.

"Beautiful," Logan whispered.

Allie glanced up at him. But he wasn't looking at the tree. He was staring at her, smiling in the glow of the Christmas lights and her stomach knotted up when she saw the look in his eyes.

"We're not going to be able to hide out from the Thompson girls for long," she finally said, when the intensity of looking into his eyes got to be too much to take.

"That's okay. I have a plan. Do you trust me?"

Allie narrowed her eyes and pretended to think about it. "Hmm…does this plan get me out of having to make any further conversation with them?"

"It does."

"In that case, I'm in."

Logan smiled and Allie's heart picked up its pace again. She was going to have to get that thing checked if this continued. "Meet me on the patio in ten minutes."

The old Logan Edwards would have jumped at the chance to spend an evening with an attractive blonde, especially one giving off signals the way Katy Thompson had been doing all evening. But he hadn't spared a second look at Katy. Sure, he'd seen the figure hugging red dress, with the slit to the top of her thigh and the neckline plunging deep into a sea of cleavage. You couldn't *not* see it.

He just wasn't interested in any of that. He didn't care enough to look again.

He'd been entirely focused on Allie.

She wore a simple black knit dress that stretched over her sizable baby bump, but also hugged the rest of her body. And he'd never known a pregnant woman could look sexy, had never really pondered it much. He'd never had reason to before. But now, he found himself captivated by the curve of her hips and the swell of her breasts. Pregnancy had supersized them.

But it was more than that. Allie was the one he wanted to

talk to tonight. She was the one he kept sharing bad puns with, and she was the one he kept exchanging looks with, every time one of the Thompsons said anything stupid. Which was often. She was the one he insisted taste his roast beef, because he'd never had roast beef that good and she hadn't put any on her plate.

She was the one he wanted to pull into his arms, and out onto the dance floor.

In hindsight, he wondered if his growing feelings for Allie had been obvious to everyone else at the table. Had Adam noticed?

He almost didn't care. It didn't matter that he'd only known her a short time. He knew her well enough to know that he'd like to know her better. He wanted to learn everything about her, every mood, every nuance, every habit. He wanted to hear every childhood story she had to tell, and watch all her favorite movies, and for her to watch all his.

Nothing like this had ever happened to him before. Could this be…could this be…something? *The* thing?

He stood by the dessert tables and waved at the woman who'd just placed a giant platter of Christmas cookies there. She was one of the owners, he thought.

"My friend isn't feeling well," he said, when he had her attention. "Is there any way I could pack up some of these desserts for her?"

"That depends. Is your friend Allie Wakeland?" the girl asked.

"That's right. How'd you know?"

"Spotted you walking in together. Allie's a friend. She helped put this place on the map. I'll pack up all the best treats and bring them to your table."

Logan winced. "What if I just wait here?"

The pretty redhead smiled. "Ah, you two are ditching Adam and the Thompson sisters, huh?"

"No. Well… kind of."

"No problem. I'll tell Adam Allie didn't feel well and you took her home. He'll believe me."

Five minutes later, Logan had their coats, a plastic container of desserts so large he thought there must be one of everything inside, and he was walking along the stone path behind Haggerty House.

The air was cool outside, but not too cold. Nothing like the cold New York winters he'd seen as a kid. Oklahoma winters were mild by comparison.

The outside of Haggerty House was magnificent. The patio opened onto a stone footpath that led to a flower garden. He bet it was spectacular in the summer, but it couldn't compare to what it looked like tonight. Hundreds of tiny white Christmas lights sparkled in the night, illuminating the walkway all the way to the garden, and twinkling from every branch and twig in it. Elegant wire reindeer grazed. A pretty pagoda, entirely twinkling, stood in the center, and Allie was sitting right there on the top step. She had her head back and her palms up.

"It's snowing," she said when he got close enough to hear.

He'd noticed a few stray flakes coming down, but hadn't thought much about it. "I take it that's rare here?"

"Not rare. But special."

She looked out over the garden covered in twinkling lights and decorations, a slight smile on her face, and he would have been content to stand there watching her for a long time. But then she shivered, just a little. He could see her breath make tiny puffs in the air and he was moving before his body consciously decided to take a step.

"I almost thought you'd changed your mind," Allie said.

"Not a chance. I just had to enlist the help of an ally." He held up the covered container of deserts as he sat down beside her on the steps.

He set the take out container down and draped Allie's coat

around her shoulders. Then he left his arm around them, too. Just couldn't convince himself to move it.

"How did you find allies in a room full of strangers?" She leaned a little closer.

"Apparently, people around here like you."

"Ah, I see. You're trading on my good name."

"Whatever it takes to impress a lovely lady."

Allie looked up at him in surprise. It was all the encouragement he needed. He brushed his lips across hers. Soft, gentle and brief. He wanted it to be more, but he didn't want to scare her away, either. She placed a hand on his chest and gave him a firm shove.

"Stop trying to charm me," she said.

"Why?"

"Because I haven't figured out why you're doing it."

"I've only just started figuring that out myself."

She blinked at him. "Really?"

"Uh-huh."

"You gonna tell me?"

He smiled. "What I've come up with so far is that it's because you're the most amazing woman I've ever met, not to mention, absolutely stunning, and drop-dead sexy."

Her eyes widened. He knew it wasn't the answer she was expecting. That was good, because he hadn't intended to say it. It wasn't a line or flattery, he meant it. He just hadn't known it until the words came out of his mouth.

He put his hand on her cheek and tilted her chin up so her eyes met his, and then his lips were on hers. He kissed her gently, sweetly, and he didn't draw back this time. There wasn't a need, because her arms wrapped around his neck. Her fingers caressed his nape and she pushed herself closer to him. His tongue darted across her lips, tracing the shape of them and feeling the silky smoothness of her mouth. He threaded his fingers through her hair and pulled her closer. She was plastered against him. Her hands raced up and down his back and he imagined how they would feel running over other parts of his body. He wanted to find out. He wanted to push her backward on the pagoda and find out exactly how much of their first encounter they could relive. He'd been remembering that night for nine long months.

He felt a strong jab in his stomach and then another. It took a second for him to realize what it was, then he looked up at Allie in surprise. "Was that...?"

She smiled. "Yeah. Your kid has great timing, huh?"

"Wow!" He was awestruck. "Is he... I mean she... I mean... always that active?"

"Not always, but a lot. Mostly when I'm trying to sleep. Here." She grabbed his hand and placed it on the side of her belly. "Feel that?"

As if on cue the baby moved, twisting beneath his hand. He wanted to stay just like that. To sit in the cold air and feel his baby move under his hands and stare at the beautiful woman in front of him and believe for just a second that things could work out for them.

The French doors on the patio opened and Logan dropped his hands, just as Adam came stalking toward them. "Lexie, I've been looking all over for you," he said.

She looked nervous. Her cheeks were rapidly turning red, but he didn't think Adam had noticed that. "You found me."

Adam's gaze cut from Allie to Logan and back again. "I just wanted to make sure you were okay. I'm taking the girls home and then I'll meet you back at your house.

"I'm fine, Adam. Really. Don't let me ruin your night. I was feeling a little queasy. That's all. Honestly, you should have fun. I already texted Angie and told her I'm on my way. I want to check on her and the kids again. It's a rough time of year for them."

Adam's eyes narrowed in suspicion as he glanced toward Logan. "And what about you?" Adam asked.

"I'm driving her." Logan smiled at Adam. "I'm still pretty jet-legged."

Adam didn't look entirely convinced, but he didn't argue.

"Fine. Text me when you get home so I know you're all right."

"Of course." Allie smiled at her brother.

"And when I get home, Lex, I think we need to have another talk about your situation." His tone was firm and Allie didn't think she was going to be able to put him off for much longer.

Adam kissed Allie on the cheek and gave his friend a searching look before turning around and returning to the restaurant.

CHAPTER NINE

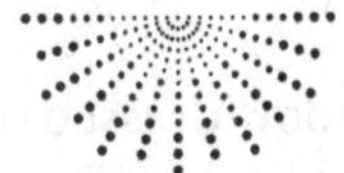

ngie's house was a brick split-level a few miles west of
Big Falls proper, near the giant construction site with
the sign that read, "Future site of Big Falls Reservoir and Park."
Lighted pine garland wound around the posts and draped from
the white railings of the small front porch. It felt like the kind of
place where weary strangers would be met at the door with a
welcoming smile, and brought inside for a cup of hot cocoa
beside a crackling fire.

They'd both been quiet on the drive. Allie didn't know what
to say. Things between them had changed. He was attentive. He
was charming. He was attracted to her and letting her know it,
and that didn't make sense.

She shivered, thinking about that kiss. It had been full of fire.
What the hell was Logan doing? He kissed her like he meant it.
Did he mean it? *Could* he mean it? Or was he just trying to
convince her that they should get married, and using every tool
at his disposal?

That had to be it, she thought. He probably thought he could
charm her into marrying him just as easily as he'd charmed her
into his arms that fateful night. And it wasn't nice, playing with

her that way, trying to make her believe there might be something real between them.

She ought to turn around and smack him, she thought as she stood at her sister's Christmassy front door, nose-to-pine cones with a wreath big enough to encircle her middle. But instead, she rang the bell and tried not to think about the man standing behind her. Her sister was more important. Holidays were hard without Jeff.

Angie came to the door dressed in fuzzy green and red stripped pajama pants and a red shirt with a sparkly Christmas tree on it. The inside of the house was dark, though it was barely eight o'clock.

Angie looked worried when she saw her little sister. "Are you okay?"

"I'm fine. Didn't you get my text?"

"No, I was busy."

"Well, I just ditched our brother and two bimbettes at Haggerty House and I wanted to check in on my way home. I didn't realize it was so late."

"It's not that late." Angie held the door open for them. "Mom and dad went home right after we got our tree up. The kids and I are watching Rudolf. Come on in. I was just about to put on some hot chocolate."

Allie stepped through the door and Logan placed a hand on the small of her back. She turned and glared at him, but not before Angie cast a curious look their way. They walked through the entryway and down a few steps into the living room. It didn't take long to see why the lights were off. Angie had the tree plugged in, and it was big enough and twinkly enough to light the whole neighborhood.

Jack was sitting in the middle of the couch, his arm around Shaggy, his sheepdog sidekick. He grabbed his remote, paused his program, and said, "Hey Logan! Come sit here."

Logan walked over to the couch and sat down and Jack

immediately began telling him about what dinosaurs he suspected might have evolved into the Bumble.

"Where's Cassie?" Allie asked her sister.

Angie looked around. "Oh no! Oh jeeze, I swear to God she was sitting right here two seconds ago!" She ran through the house, and Allie followed. The dining room was dark, but the kitchen light was on. They both raced through the doorway and skidded to a stop. Cassie sat in front of the fridge, exactly as she had before at Allie's house. A dozen eggs lay smashed around her on the floor. This time she held a spatula in her hand and was slapping it repeatedly in the egg-puddle, sending yolk-spatter in a hundred directions.

"Eggs. It's always eggs." Angie scooped up the little girl and handed her to Allie.

Allie took her, grasping under the arms. The kid was dripping in egg. "She does this often?"

"Every chance she gets."

Relief washed through Allie in a rush that left her knees weak. She hadn't even realized how bad she'd been feeling about the egg incident until it just whooshed away, leaving her lighter than before. "Why didn't you tell me?"

Angie sent her a puzzled frown. "It never came up. She sticks string beans up her nose, and puts pancakes in the DVD player, too."

Allie felt like she might cry. "I thought it was just me. I couldn't keep her out of trouble even for a couple hours." She pulled Cassie right in close. To heck with the sticky, gooey mess on her hands and clothes. She hugged her. Cassie grabbed a handful of hair with an egg-coated hand. "She got into my eggs, too."

"I knew something had happened," Angie said. "No, sis, it's not you. She does this. A lot. I can barely blink. But at least it's just eggs. She's not getting outside or sticking forks into electrical outlets or—"

"Oh, God." The horror of that notion ended Allie's relief instantly. "I don't think I'm ready for this." Allie whispered the words she'd been afraid to say, even to herself. "Angie, what am I gonna do? I don't know how to be a mommy."

"Oh sweetie, *nobody* is ready for this. It doesn't matter who you are, how old you are, married or single, planned or unplanned. Nothing can prepare anyone for motherhood—except motherhood." She grabbed a roll of paper towels from under the sink. "The good news is, it starts slow. At first, they're so little the worst thing they do is cry. Other than that, they eat, sleep and snuggle. The crying can be tough, and the lack of sleep is brutal for a couple of months, but the snuggling is worth the trouble." She kissed Cassie's cheek, then bent to clean up the egg mess.

"I don't know. I don't know." Allie gazed at her niece and tried to imagine living up to the love and trust in her eyes.

"You learn as you go, you figure out what they need, and you fall in love with them. Head over heels. So by the time they start doing things like this, you love them enough that you don't go completely insane."

Allie plucked a piece of eggshell out of her niece's beautiful blond hair. "How do you do it on your own, Angie? I don't think I'm strong enough."

Angie pushed puddles of egg around the floor, trying to capture them in the paper towels. Globs kept escaping.

"When you have no other choice, you get strong in a hurry." She tossed the wad of paper towels into the garbage can and grabbed another bunch. "But…" Angie bit her lower lip. "I'll shut up."

"But what?" Allie asked. "Go on, tell me."

She shrugged one shoulder. "Are you sure you have no other choice?"

Allie shook her head. "I'm not sure of anything."

"Well, I don't know what's going on with you, mostly

because you stubbornly refuse to spill it. I understand that. Mostly. But just think about it. I'm not saying you need to marry the guy or even date him, but if he's around and he's willing to be involved, let him. Because if you don't—babies grow up, Allie. This baby will be Cassie's age, and then Jack's age, and then a teenager and then an adult. Sooner or later, you're gonna have to answer all the questions from 'who is my father,' to 'why isn't he in my life?'"

A big hot tear erupted, and rolled slowly down Allie's cheek. Cassie patted it with her gooey hand. "I'm gonna go start the tub."

"I knew I should've shut up," Angie muttered as she hurried away.

~

"If I were Rudolph, I'd fly a quetzalcoatlus in there to get the Bumble," Jack said.

"What's a quetzalcoatlus?"

"It's a pterosaur and it was the biggest flying animal of all time."

"You mean like a pterodactyl?"

"That's not their real name. 'Member? I 'splained that to you last time."

"Okay, so you say Rudolph should just use the quetzalco-whatsit, but what if Rudolph doesn't have a ..." Logan trailed off as Allie entered the room, a sticky messy toddler wriggling and giggling in her arms.

Allie drew his focus, no matter where they were or who else was present. His eyes just stopped obeying his brain when she walked into a room.

She was smiling adoringly at the little girl in her arms. There was something sticky in her hair and on her face, and all over little Cassie. For a second he thought about their own baby in those same arms. Or in his. The dog jumped off the couch and ran to the kitchen, apparently recognizing the signs of a food-coated floor, and eager to help clean up Cassie's mess.

"It's a quetz-al-co-at-lus." Jack said the worlds slowly, forcing Logan's attention back to him. Allie disappeared with the sticky baby, and he heard water running somewhere nearby. "If Rudolph doesn't have one, he should get in his time machine and go get one."

Logan nodded. "Sure, but what if he doesn't have a time machine?"

Jack rolled his eyes. "He lives in the North Pole. With Santa. He could definitely get a time machine."

Logan didn't even try to argue with that logic.

They spent a few minutes just watching the show. "I don't understand the *Island of Misfit Toys*," Logan said after a little while. "What's wrong with that doll? She looks normal to me."

Jack gave him a look like he thought Logan had the mentality of an ant. "You know it's just pretend, right?"

"Are you sure?"

"Can you keep a secret?" Jack's tone was serious.

"Of course."

Jack leaned a little closer. "Santa's not real."

Logan didn't know what to say. He didn't have any experience dealing with kids, but he was pretty sure this wasn't a discussion he should be having. This was something Jack should talk to his mother about. He was afraid he was going to say the wrong thing. Pretty sure of it actually, because he couldn't think of anything to say at all.

"Why do you say that?" he asked, deciding non-committal was his best bet.

"Last year, I was really good, and I only asked Santa for one thing, and I didn't get it. I *always* get the stuff I ask for if you can buy it at the store, but if Santa was real, he could help with the *important* stuff, too."

Logan didn't have to ask Jack what he meant. He remembered Allie's story. The kid had been sure Santa would bring his dad home for Christmas last year.

Logan put his arm around Jack's shoulders. "Some problems are so big, even Santa can't fix them, buddy," Logan said. "But that doesn't mean you should give up on him."

Jack shrugged. "You wouldn't understand."

"I do understand. I don't have any parents."

"Everybody has parents," Jack said in his knowing voice.

"I guess that's true, but I never knew mine. They gave me away when I was little and I spent lots of Christmases asking Santa for a family. And when it didn't happen, I was sure he wasn't real. Just like you are now."

"So, I'm right."

"No, I don't think so. I don't think I was either." The look in the little boy's eyes made Logan's heart break. It was like his last shred of hope was vanishing.

"Santa might not be able to fix everything, but I believe he's real. There's something magical about Christmastime. People start looking out for each other and doing nice things for each other, and let me tell you kid, that doesn't happen every day. That's real magic—the best *kind* of magic. It's the kind that you can trick yourself into thinking isn't real. But it's the most real kind of all, Jack. Because it's not just toys and presents. It's something a lot harder to make. Something that matters."

Logan knew Allie was standing behind him. He didn't know how long she'd been there, but he knew she was listening.

"Everybody says he's gone and he's not coming back, but do you think the magic could be strong enough to bring my dad home this year?" Jack didn't meet Logan's eyes when he asked it. Logan knew he should say no. He didn't want Jack to be holding out hope again, only to be destroyed Christmas morning. He couldn't bear the thought of that, but he couldn't be the one to destroy the little guy's last hope either.

"I don't know, Jack. What I do know is if your daddy could be here with you, he would be. And he wouldn't want you to stop believing in magic just because he didn't make it home."

Jack nodded. He turned his head back toward the television, but his arm snaked around Logan's and he rested his cheek against his shoulder. Logan couldn't help but notice the tears that dripped onto his shirt where the little boy's head hung, but he pretended not to. Jack's little shoulders shook and Logan squeezed the little boy closer to his side.

Allie came around the side of the couch, her own eyes were damp. She mouthed a silent thank you and sat down in the spot that the dog had vacated. Logan's fingers found Allie's, and without letting go of the little boy, he held her hand.

Logan wondered about their child. He prayed their baby would never have to go through what Jack was going through. He knew this was Allie's reason. It was why she didn't want to try to have a future with him, and he couldn't blame her. He'd spent hours with this little boy and his heart broke for him. He couldn't imagine Allie, knowing what Jack had gone through, what their own child might face if things went wrong, and still taking a chance on a relationship with him. The situation seemed hopeless, but her fingers were warm against his. He hoped this could be the start of a future for them. But how could it be? In less than two weeks, he'd be flying back to Afghanistan. How was he supposed to make things work with her when he only had twelve days to do it?

Angie stepped out of the bathroom with Cassie in her arms. The little girl was dressed in Grinch footie pajamas and she looked the picture of innocence as she yawned against her mother's shoulder. "You two might have to visit every night," she said in a hushed voice. "It usually takes me hours to get Jack down."

Allie squeezed his fingers and let go of his hand and he knew it was because she didn't want her sister to know there might be something between them.

"He's had nightmares ever since..."

Logan stood, scooping the little boy into his arms. "He'll be okay. It just takes time," he gave Angie a reassuring smile. "Where should I put him?"

"Follow me," Allie said.

She led the way up the stairs to the entryway and then up another set to the second level. A nightlight lit the hall and he followed Allie to the end of it. She opened Jack's door and hurried inside to pull back the covers on his bed. Logan walked carefully, trying to avoid the toys that were scattered on the floor. His foot slammed into a robot and it started talking and flashing lights. He held his breath for a second, hoping the noise wouldn't wake Jack.

The little boy stirred and wrapped his arms tighter around Logan's neck. He snuggled close. "Daddy," he muttered in a sleepy voice. Logan felt his heart crack in his chest all over again. He lay the little boy down in his bed and tucked the blankets around his shoulders.

Allie's little farmhouse was quiet when they pulled into the driveway. Adam's car was nowhere in sight and Allie thanked her lucky stars for that. She loved her brother, but a little more alone time with Logan wasn't unwelcome. Maybe he'd explain himself, or admit the truth, or....kiss her again.

What harm could it do? She was already pregnant.

But she knew that would lead to more complications. She wasn't ready to plan a happily ever after with him, and she knew that would only make her more confused about what was happening between them.

The coward in her wanted to sneak off to bed, but she didn't think she'd get any sleep with him in the next room. She'd be thinking about that kiss every time she closed her eyes.

Logan didn't look at all bothered by the situation. He closed the door behind her after she let them both in, and then he walked into the kitchen. She took off her coat, and heeled off her shoes, stretched her back, and then went further inside to see what he was up to. He had a plate of cookies and had poured milk for two.

He gave her that mischievous grin that made her toes curl. She didn't return it.

"Are you unhappy with my snack selection?"

"Not on your life."

He set the glasses down on the kitchen island and moved closer to her. "Are you unhappy with something else I've done?"

"No."

"Then maybe you're unhappy because of something I haven't done yet." He moved closer still until he was mere inches away from her. His fingers trailed over the side of her face, pushing a lock of hair behind her ear. "Is that it?"

Her head was suddenly clouded with thoughts of him. Of what could happen between them.

"You don't really want me. You couldn't. Stop pretending."

"Allie, I told you, you have no idea what I want. And if you think I don't want you, you're fooling yourself. Do you know how many nights I spent alone dreaming of having you this close to me again?" He twisted a lock of her hair around his finger, rubbing it with his thumb. "I've never wanted anyone as much as I want you right now."

She closed her eyes, wishing she could believe him.

"I could prove it to you."

Her breath caught in her throat. He leaned down to kiss her and all her fears and doubts came to the forefront. His lips brushed across hers, and she felt panic settling in. She slid a hand onto his chest between them and pushed him gently.

"We can't... You're leaving soon. This isn't smart."

He sighed and looked down at her with a sad smile. "That's what I thought you'd say. Hence the cookies." He shrugged, gave a sad smile. "So, do you want to take 'em to the couch and watch a movie?"

"Just because I'm pregnant, you assume I want cookies?" She made her tone teasing, to hide the storm going on inside her.

"No, *I* want cookies. But I'm willing to share. If you don't want any, I'm more than happy to eat them myself. You make some damn good cookies."

She smiled. "Don't be silly. I always want cookies." She turned and headed into the living room, sank onto the sofa and reached for the remote. "We can each them while we watch *White Christmas.*

Logan brought the cookies and milk and sat down beside her. She was eager to watch her favorite holiday movie, and more eager to watch it with him. But when he sat down beside her and put his arm around her shoulders, she had a hard time concentrating on the television screen.

Logan didn't seem to be having the same problem.

"The Army must have been a lot different in the forties. No one in my unit has ever preformed a song and dance number while taking mortar fire."

Allie smiled. "Maybe if you hadn't come home before Christmas, you would have seen some kind of a show."

"Maybe," he said.

It felt good, sitting beside him, eating cookies, watching him enjoy the film. She told herself not to get used to having Logan around. The more she let herself enjoy this now, the worse she would feel when he was gone. And yet, she couldn't stop herself from snuggling closer and leaning her head on his shoulder, and before she knew it, she was fast asleep.

~

"What the hell do you think you're doing, Edwards?" Adam's voice pulled Logan out of a sound sleep. The first decent sleep he'd had since coming home.

He was tired and groggy and it took him a minute to figure out why Adam was so upset. But once his brain started firing on all cylinders, he realized that the reason he was so warm and comfortable was because Allie was snuggled up at his side. Her head was cradled on his chest and his chin had been resting on the top of her head.

Logan placed a finger to his lips and struggled to untangle himself. It took some effort. Allie's fingers were wrapped around the collar of his shirt, and she didn't seem in any hurry to let go.

Adam stood there, apparently seething.

He finally managed to roll Allie away from him and he stood up and walked into the dining room. Adam followed.

"What is going on with you and my sister?" Adam wasn't speaking in best-friend tones. He was 100% in C.O. mode.

Logan wanted to tell the truth. This was his chance. His friend was asking him a question and he didn't want to lie. But all he could see in his mind was Allie's eyes as she'd begged him to keep the secret for just a little longer. He couldn't betray her now.

"Look, she's…she's an amazing woman. She needs someone to lean on right now and I don't mind being there for her," he said instead.

Adam looked at Logan for a long time. When he spoke, he was calmer, but just as firm. "She's in a fragile state. Maybe you're just trying to be a good guy, but it would be easy for her to get confused right now. She can't handle someone else coming into her life and then taking off again just when she needs them. Not again."

It was like a knife to his chest, but Logan knew Adam was right. He hadn't intended to leave Allie to handle an entire pregnancy on her own, but he had. And he was going to do it again only this time she would be left to handle a baby.

"I just want to help her while I can. That's all."

Deep down, though, he had to admit that helping Allie wasn't his true motivation. Part of it, yeah. But being with Allie made him feel better than he'd felt in a long time. Maybe it was selfish, but when he was around her, he didn't feel like an orphaned kid in search of a family.

He felt like a whole person. He felt complete.

"That sounds noble, Logan, but I swear to God, if you end up hurting her, I'll make your life a living hell."

If he hurt her, Logan thought, Adam wouldn't have to make him miserable, because he'd already be there.

Adam paced out of the room and back to the couch. He shook Allie's shoulder and she woke with a start. "It's just me, Lexie. I think it's time for you to get to bed."

Allie muttered unintelligibly, stood up and shuffled her feet to the stairs and up them, to her bedroom.

Logan followed her up, and headed into the guest room, knowing Adam was still at the foot of the stairs watching. He wanted to walk right back out the door and into Allie's room. He wanted to hold her in his arms and fall asleep with his body pressed tight against hers, but he knew that would only cause her trouble, so instead, he punched the pillow on the hard futon and looked forward to another night of tossing and turning.

CHAPTER TEN

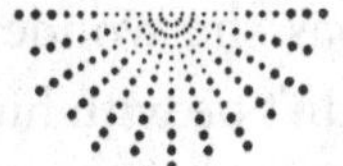

3 DAYS BEFORE CHRISTMAS

*A*llie woke up alone. Her bed felt huge and empty and cold. All night, she had dreamed about that kiss in the fairy light pavilion outside Haggerty House. She'd replayed it in her mind over and over, and now that she was awake, she was still replaying it. Reliving it.

She knew what Logan was doing. He was trying to make her fall for him.

This was stupid. She couldn't fall for Logan. He would be gone in two weeks. Less! Marriage to a soldier was the one thing she *didn't* want. She wouldn't put her child through it. She wouldn't put herself through it.

God, poor Angie. And Jack—Jack broke her heart.

She wondered if Logan was up yet, then wondered why she was wondering. Then she sat up in bed and listened for sounds from his room. It was silent and she hoped that meant he was still asleep. She needed to get out of here and find a place where she could have some solitude and a cup of fake coffee.

She crept out of bed, grabbed some clothes from her closet and tiptoed into the bathroom for a quick shower. And the whole time her mind was churning. What was Logan offering here, anyway? What did he have in mind?

What did he plan to do after his deployment? Would he'd be stationed nearby? Did he plan to re-enlist when his time was up? And what did he want from her? Did he want a real marriage—a relationship with her, romance, regular sex, the whole shebang? Or did he just want a paper marriage, for the baby's sake? And why was she wondering all that, when she'd already decided she couldn't be with him?

Her entire life was about to change, and starting a relationship—a real one, with a husband, for God's sake—didn't seem like the smartest idea. It was just bad timing. How much change could she handle all at once?

And what if they tried and failed? What would a divorce do to the baby?

She'd hoped the shower would clear her mind, but twenty minutes later she'd put on a dress and dried her hair, and she was still had no answers.

She sighed, tiptoeing out of the bathroom, and down to the living room. She grabbed a pair of ballet flats and shoved her feet into them, grateful that she didn't have to mess with laces. She was putting on a jacket when she heard footsteps on the stairs. Logan came quietly down, wearing jeans and a long-sleeved thermal shirt the color of cranberries. He was still yards away, but she could smell the faint trace of his cologne and it made her heart beat a little faster.

"What the—are you *leaving*?"

"How the heck do you hear me every time I try to sneak out?" she asked in a loud whisper.

"Because you're in the room next to mine and I'm sleeping with one eye open in case you go into labor. Are you *really leaving* me here to deal with Adam on my own?"

"Are you *really* too scared to face him by yourself?"

"Course not." He shrugged. "He'll probably murder me and

throw my body out for the coyotes. But I'm prepared to face it like a man."

"I hate to miss all that, but I have a doctor's appointment, so I have no choice." She patted her belly bump. "Gotta do what's best for the baby."

He crossed his arms over his chest and leaned on the newel post. "I know I'm new to this, but do they regularly schedule those for six a.m.?"

"I like to be punctual." She shot a look at the closed door to the den and hoped they wouldn't wake her brother.

"Bull."

He was right and he knew it. She had two hours before the appointment, but she didn't want to be here, and he was the reason why.

He crossed the room, stopping a few feet shy of her. "Don't… fathers…usually go along, for these kinds of things?"

Allie's pulse sped up. This felt too real, this concern of his, this wanting to be involved, this devotion. For a second she could imagine that they were a normal couple, doing this the normal way. That he would be there to help her through everything from now on. But that idealistic image rippled and faded when the usual questions came rushing back. Who knew what tomorrow would bring? He might disappear after the holidays and never come back. He might show up on birthdays and holidays and nothing more. He might get shipped halfway around the world. He might hit an IED like her brother-in-law did.

"What would we tell Adam?" she whispered. God, was she actually considering letting him come with her?

Logan rolled his eyes. "I love your brother, but I'm sick of watching everything I say and do because of what he might think. He's going to figure this out eventually, and when he does, I think he'd be happier knowing that I was trying to be involved than he would be if I shirked my fatherly duties. Besides, I *want* to go with you."

"I don't know," Allie said. She wanted to keep whatever this was with Logan under the radar. She wanted to put off telling Adam until after the baby was born, if she had to tell him at all. "Hell, I left my purse in my room." She hurried up the stairs, back to her bedroom to grab her purse, but stopped in the hallway outside Logan's room. The door was open, and there on the nightstand was her copy of *What to Expect When You're Expecting*. A bookmark stuck out the top, and Allie was quite sure that she hadn't put it there. Her heart swelled, and even though she tried to ignore it, she felt herself melt a little bit. She got her bag, and headed back down.

He was standing right where she'd left him, waiting near the front door. "Okay," she said. "You can come with me."

First, they went to Sunny's Place. Sunny herself unlocked the door to let them in, despite the CLOSED sign still hanging in the window. She looked like the picture they would put in the dictionary beside the word "Sunny."

"I'm sorry I'm here before hours," Allie said. "I just needed—"

"Fresh brewed decaf and a great big cream-filled, chocolate-frosted donut?" Sunny blinked her big Bambi eyes.

Allie smiled as if in bliss. "You read my mind."

"Take a spot in the back, Allie. The CLOSED sign will stay up for another twenty minutes, so you can have all the solitude you need to go with that breakfast." Then she smiled right at Logan. "Hi, again."

"Nice to see you again."

They each had a mugful of the best coffee on planet Earth, and sat across from each other, and said almost nothing. Logan had tried to start a conversation once, but she'd just held up a finger, then returned to her former position, leaning back in her seat, eyes closed, eating her donut as slowly as humanly possible

So, he'd kept quiet and let her enjoy her sweet breakfast. And he'd kind of fallen into the peace of it too, after a bit, and thoroughly enjoyed his own.

And then they walked back to the car and drove to Doc Sophie's.

A fancy sign on the front lawn of the white Victorian said "Big Falls Family Clinic." It was a three-person operation from what he could tell. There was a grandmotherly receptionist, who'd had Allie sign in, and asked them to take a seat in the waiting room. There was a pretty red-haired nurse, who came out to say, "Allie, you can come on back, now." And there was, presumably, a doctor they'd see at some point.

"This is my friend Logan," Allie said. As he followed her out of the waiting room, through a door and down a short hall. "He's here for moral support and if anyone hears about it, it would cause a lot of trouble. So—"

"For us, too," the nurse said. "It'd be a privacy violation. Don't worry. You're secret's safe with us." She led them into an exam room, where a paper-covered, padded table awaited.

Logan was nervous as hell, and had no idea what he was doing here. All he knew was that there was something about Allie that made him want to get close and stay close. He couldn't describe the way he felt when he was around her. It wasn't just attraction. Although he was attracted to her, which was probably weird since she was so very, *very* pregnant. But there was more to it than that. He was compelled to protect her, take care of her. She made him feel settled, almost anchored, in a way he'd never felt before. Maybe it was because she was carrying his child. His own flesh and blood child. Right there, inside her.

The nurse—he finally dragged his eyes off Allie long enough to catch a look at her name tag—Barbie Bennett, R.N.—checked Allie's vital signs, then said, "Okay, step up on the scale."

Allie gave Logan a pointed look. He smiled at her, and

turned around, putting his back to the scale. He heard the springs moving as she stepped on.

"Any pain or bleeding since your last appointment?" Barbie Bennett R.N. asked.

"Everything is perfectly normal," Allie said. "Except I'm incredibly impatient, short tempered, and getting kind of antsy."

"That's normal, too. Good signs, actually." She made a few notes in her chart.

The door opened and another woman came in. She was tall, blond, and smiling, and she took the chart from the nurse but kept her eyes on her patient. "Hi, Allie." And then she turned to him. "Hello, Sergeant Edwards. Welcome home." She extended a hand. "I'm Dr. McIntyre, but most everyone calls me Doc Sophie."

"How did you know who I was?" He asked, shaking her small, strong hand.

"Small town. Everybody knows who you are." She turned her attention to the chart, then. "How's our girl doing?"

"Her blood pressure is a little high," the nurse replied.

"Have you been under stress lately, Allie?" Doc Sophie asked.

"Oh, you know, just the usual stuff. Holiday time. Family in town. Houseguests."

Logan sent her a worried look. She looked tired. Her eyes weren't as bright as usual. Why hadn't he noticed sooner?

Doc Sophie jotted a few more notes on the chart and said, "Can you give us a minute, Barb?"

Nodding, Barbie hurried from the room. The doc then directed her attention to Logan. "So, keeping in mind that I can't say anything outside this room, are you the father?"

Logan looked at Allie, telling her without a word that the decision about how much to admit was all hers. Allie held his eyes a long moment, then looked at the Doc and nodded. Logan sighed in such abject relief he couldn't believe it. It felt good to just be honest about it with somebody.

"He was deployed," Allie explained. "He just got home."

"Just in time, too. That's good, because I'm putting you in charge of keeping her relaxed. No stress. Think you can do that?"

"I'll do my best," Logan said. It would be a challenge. "Is this blood pressure thing dangerous? Should we be worried?"

"It's usually nothing serious. If it goes any higher, we'll want to run some tests."

Logan felt nerves swirl in his stomach. He'd read something about what high BP was a sign of in the pregnancy book, but he couldn't remember what it had said. "What tests? What would you be looking for?"

"It's high blood pressure, Logan, not a brain tumor," Allie said. "Don't make me sorry I let you come."

"It's nothing to worry about," Doc Sophie said. "And the point here is that you need to stay *calm*. Both of you."

Allie didn't look worried. Logan wasn't sure how that was possible, when he felt terrified that there might be something wrong, but she looked completely at ease.

"I'll be right back," Doc Sophie said, and she left them alone.

As soon as the door closed, Allie sighed and said, "Don't worry, Logan. I'm healthy and young. Women have babies every day. It's going to be fine."

He tried to focus on her words instead of the crazy possibilities whirling in his head, but it was hard to make the panic go away.

A second later, the doc came back through the doors wheeling a cart full of electronics and a monitor. "We don't usually do this unless it's medically necessary, but I thought since Sergeant Edwards missed the official ultrasound..."

Apparently knowing the drill, Allie laid back on the exam table and pulled a sheet over her lower body, then pushed up her blouse, exposing her belly. It was so full of baby that her belly button had turned inside out.

"Remember, Doc, I like surprises. Especially at Christmas. So don't tell me anything about gender."

"You've got it." The doc was flipping switches. She squeezed neon blue gel in an *s* pattern on Allie's belly, then pressed a sensor to her and moved it slowly around. An image appeared on the computer screen, but it was dark and grainy and Logan had no idea what he was seeing. A blob of light pulsed on the screen and the doctor clicked a few buttons and made some notes. "That," she said, pointing to the blinking light "is your baby's heartbeat."

"Oh my God," he whispered. And then he said it again. His hand found Allie's and he moved closer to her side. Suddenly it was real. They had made a baby.

Doc Sophie moved the little sensor and made a few more notes before pointing at the screen again. "Do you know what you're looking at?"

Logan stared at the screen for a second. He couldn't see anything at first. Shapes, light and shadow. But then suddenly the blurry object started to take shape, like one of those 3D puzzles. Once he saw it, he couldn't see anything else. "Is that... the baby's face?"

Sophie nodded, and Logan's heart seemed to expand in his chest. He couldn't keep from smiling, not that he tried. He was sure he looked like a blithering idiot, but he didn't care. There was a rounded cheek and a little button nose, and then the baby raised a tiny fist.

"A little thumb sucking," Doc Sophie said with a delighted smile. She clicked a few more buttons and the machine on the cart printed a picture. Then she took the sensor off and wiped away the goo. "Allie, I'll be back in a moment for your exam, but so far, everything looks wonderful." She handed Logan the picture and left the room, pulling the door closed behind her.

Logan helped Allie sit up and pressed a light kiss to her forehead. He stared at the little face in the picture and then at her belly. Any day now, that tiny baby was going to make its way into the world.

And he was going to have to leave soon after.

The disappointment of that realization hit him harder than it had before. He couldn't imagine ever wanting to leave, but he didn't have a choice and he had no idea if Allie would be waiting for him when he came back.

He looked at Allie, and suddenly understood why she didn't want to marry him. That disappointment, that feeling of heartache, of missing someone so much and being unable to do anything about it, that was what she was trying to protect herself from. And what she was trying to protect their baby from.

Maybe he shouldn't be fighting her so hard.

"I don't want to talk to Santa."

It was later that same afternoon. Allie and Logan stood in the middle of the town's circular park. She'd been trying to convince Jack to go talk to the man in red, who held court in a pavilion near the giant, decorated Christmas tree.

"Come on, Jack," she said. "Your mom would love a picture of you and Cassie with Santa. It will be our Christmas surprise for her."

"You know he's not the real Santa, right?" Jack whispered at her. "If there is a real Santa, it's not this guy."

Allie scanned the line of kids behind them to make sure no one else had heard. Since no one had broken down in a fit of tears, she figured they were safe. Logan was holding Cassie on his hip, and she was wriggling and twisting to free herself. She couldn't wait to get to Santa.

Logan shifted her a little, knelt beside Jack and said something in a conspiratorial whisper.

"Fine. I'll see him," Jack said.

Allie felt her heart warm toward Logan a little more. In a few short days, he'd managed to win over Jack, and she wasn't sure what she would have done if he hadn't been there.

That was the problem really, because she knew he wouldn't be for much longer.

A family exited the pavilion and a teenage girl dressed as an elf ushered them up the steps. Jack stopped at the top and refused to budge.

A very convincing Santa sat in a throne-like chair in the center.

"Don't be shy, Jack. I've been waiting for you," he said. His eyes twinkled. Jack met them, and a little frown creased his forehead. Allie took his hand and crossed the room, Logan right behind her, carrying Cassie until the little girl twisted free, hit the floor running, and raced right up to the old man with her arms out, calling "Santa! Santa!"

He scooped her up and she released a happy squeal.

Jack held back, pressing closer to Logan's side.

Santa held out his white-gloved hand, crooked his fingers toward him in a come-here gesture.

"I'm just here to take a picture for my mom. You can't bring me what I want for Christmas." Jack looked at the floor and Allie kicked herself for thinking this was a good idea.

"Well now, we'll see about that," Santa said, "But first, let's get the photography out of the way, all right?"

Jack wiped his eyes dry and crossed the distance between them. The elf grabbed the camera, not that it mattered, Allie had brought her own. She pulled it out of the bag, but Santa held up a hand for them to wait. He placed his gloved hand over Jack's on the arm of his chair. Cassie was snuggled up on his other knee, her head resting against Santa's deep red velvet coat. She looked like an angel.

"Jack, listen. A lot of people stop believing in me if they don't get the things they want right away. But I don't want you to give up hope. Not ever. The gifts that really matter, those take time."

Allie cleared her throat, wanting to get the man's attention, wanting to tell him not to give Jack false hope. She didn't want Jack to be heartbroken on Christmas morning for the second year in a row. But Santa just looked at her and smiled.

"Some wishes take years and years before they come true. Ask your friend there. How long have you been waiting for me to fulfill your Christmas wish, Sergeant Edwards?" Santa was looking at Logan now.

Logan didn't say anything, but a funny expression crossed his face and his eyes darted to Allie and then away.

"But Logan never got what he asked for."

Santa leaned closer and whispered in Jack's ear, and Jack's mouth fell open. The anger and sadness left his eyes.

"Will I get what I asked for this year?" Jack asked. His eyes were more hopeful than they'd been in a long time.

"Santa," Allie said in a warning voice, but the man waved her off with a smile.

"The important things take more time, like I said. But you must keep hoping, Jack. You must keep believing. And sooner or later, your wish will come true. Never give up. No matter what anyone tells you. Just keep looking forward and knowing."

Jack no longer looked upset, and while that was good for the moment, Allie was worried about how her nephew would react on Christmas morning. She was going to start planning for the worst now and she knew that meant she was going to have to tell her sister about this little trip. She just hoped it wouldn't be the thing her nephew told his therapist about for the next thirty years.

Santa turned toward the cameras, and Jack sat on the arm of his chair and smiled. The elf's camera flashed once. Allie snapped several shots. This gift was definitely not worth the trouble, she thought as she scooped Cassie from Santa's arms.

The little girl kicked and wriggled. Her arms stretched out to the jolly old man.

Santa laughed and handed each of the kids a candy cane. Cassie babbled sweetly at him. He whispered something in Jack's ear, then gave him a wink.

"Your photo will be ready in an hour," said the elf, as she ushered them toward the door.

They crossed Main street, which split around the park like a river around a boulder, to the Big Falls Diner for hot chocolate and sugary treats while they waited for their pictures, and Allie couldn't deny that Jack was in a much better mood than he had been before.

They walked back over to the park an hour later. Cassie was now sound asleep on Logan's shoulder. The pictures were in a plastic bin on a table to the side of Santa's pavilion. Allie and Jack began flipping through the photos to find theirs.

"Aunt Allie, look," Jack said excitedly. He held up a photo of the family that had come out of the pavilion before they had entered.

"Jack, those are someone else's pictures. Put them back."

"But *look*, Aunt Allie. It's not the same Santa."

Allie looked closer and saw that Jack was right. The Santa in this picture wore a suit that was a lighter red, and sported a long, curling, silky white beard.

"Well, sometimes Santa needs help."

"I know all that. But look at this." Jack pulled out the next picture in the pile. The picture of him and Cassie and the much more believable Santa Claus. He had a real beard, gray and white and silver, and just the right length. His suit was darker, and you could make out swirls and symbols, barely visible in the deep red velvet. Then Jack pulled out the picture behind it and showed Allie another shot of the Santa with the fake beard. "He's only in *our* picture. *We* saw the *real* Santa!"

She tried to think of a logical explanation for it. It was

possible the pictures weren't in order. The Santas might be working in shifts. Maybe they had just caught them when they switched. She wanted to flip through a few more pictures in the bin, but other families were waiting to collect their photos.

Maybe he had just filled in while the other Santa took a bathroom break. That was reasonable. But it didn't explain how Santa had seemed to know what was bothering Jack. Or his name. Or Logan's name.

It's a small town. Everybody knows who you are. Doc Sophie's statement was obviously true.

Logan leaned in close, Cassie asleep on his shoulder. He said, "We have to go."

Nodding, she followed behind, watching Logan with Cassie and Jack holding his hand and all but skipping along beside him.

"What was he talking about?" she asked Logan quietly when they got to the car. Jack was buckling himself up, and Logan was installing Cassie in the car seat in the back. "What did you ask for," Allie whispered. "The year you stopped believing in Santa? What was the gift he couldn't bring you that year?"

He snapped the buckles, closed the door, looked at her with eyes that were sparkling with almost as much childlike wonder and Christmas magic as Jack's were now.

"A family," he told her. Then he glanced at the photos she held and said, "You better hold onto those. Not too many people have photographic proof of the real Santa Claus."

CHAPTER ELEVEN

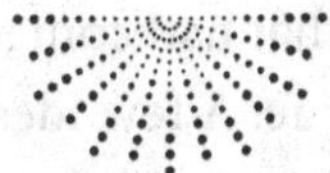

2 DAYS BEFORE CHRISTMAS

*A*ny day now. That's what Doc Sophie had said after her internal exam. Any day now. But apparently, not today. Which was good, because Allie was going to a wedding.

Her friend and mentor, Edie Brand Armstrong, had come down with a stomach bug and had to cancel on a wedding she'd planned to photograph today, and the bride to be had phoned Allie on the edge of hysteria. Nobody thought it was a good idea that she take on the job. Even Allie didn't think it was the best idea. But the ceremony was out by the falls, and would be short and sweet, and if she could just get those photos, the young bride said, that would be enough. She had plenty of guests with cell phones to shoot the reception.

It shouldn't have taken long, but of course, it did.

And it turned out that being around two people who were head over heels in love, while they said their vows with tears in their eyes, and sealed their promise with a kiss, wasn't the best way to avoid thinking about her and Logan.

She barely kept herself from crying through the entire event.

She took a lot of beautiful shots, capturing emotion that would leap right out of the photos. But the entire time, she'd been thinking about Logan and the baby they were going to bring into this world any day now. And she'd been wishing there was something she could do to keep him from leaving in another week. Because she couldn't be with him if he was going to leave her. And she wanted to be with him.

That was the conclusion she'd come to. She wanted to be with him. But she couldn't.

So far, no solution to that had come to mind.

That wasn't entirely true. A few ideas had come to her. She'd considered running him over with her car, or breaking his legs with a baseball bat. They couldn't very well ship him back to Afghanistan if he couldn't walk.

When she got home after the longer-than-planned after-noon, she parked her car on the side of the road in front of her house, because her driveway was full. Her parents were there. Angie was there and Adam was home, which meant she was going to have to go in and pretend that nothing was out of the ordinary, even though she felt like her heart was being pulled to pieces.

She plastered a smile on her face, climbed out of the car and walked inside.

Her house was full of laugher and noise, like it always was when the family was visiting, but when Allie walked in, she didn't see a single person.

The sound of Christmas music and laughter was coming from upstairs, so Allie followed it up and into the guest room.

It smelled like fresh paint. Light and voices and music spilled out the partially open door and Allie pushed it open the rest of the way. And then her breath caught in her throat. The walls were freshly painted in the soft green she'd chosen. The crib was set up where the futon had been only a few hours earlier. The changing table had been assembled too, and now it held rows of diapers and stacks of baby wipes. A brand-new rocking chair sat on the left side of the room near the big window, with thick yellow cushions. Tiny Christmas lights had been strung around the ceiling.

She looked around the room from one person to the next. Her parents smiled at her from the window where her mom was placing curtains on the rod and handing them to her dad to hang. Little Jack was folding tiny outfits and putting them in the baby's dresser and Cassie was unfolding them and holding them up and saying, "oooo, pwetty." Adam was hanging pictures of happy animals on the walls, and Angie was just finishing up the fresh white paint on the woodwork. And there, in the middle of it all, was Logan. He stood by the crib, adjusting the mobile over top of it, and the look on his face brought tears to her eyes.

"Surprise!" her mom said.

"What do you think?" Adam asked.

"This is incredible! Thank you. All of you." She looked at Logan and hoped he knew she was talking to him. "How did you get this all done? I've only been gone a few hours."

"Logan started long before we got here," Allie's mom told her. The paint's still a little tacky, but we thought it was dry enough to add the finishing touches."

The doorbell rang.

"Pizza's here," Adam said, clapping his hands together. The hungry hoard all but stampeded out of the room and downstairs to greet the pizza guy, leaving Allie alone with Logan.

"This was your idea?" she asked.

"I didn't see how we'd get it all done without help, and Doc Sophie did say any day now."

"I thought it was odd nobody insisted on chaperoning me today."

"Your mother asked the mother of the bride to keep an eye on you."

"Of course she did."

He smiled. "Of course she did."

Allie closed the distance between them and threw her arms around his neck. "Thank you."

Logan lowered his mouth to hers and kissed her, and everything else, even the fact that her entire family was only a short flight of stairs away from them, just evaporated from her mind. She couldn't think of anything at all except for him.

Eventually, though, she ended the kiss, and stared up at him, knowing her heart was probably in her eyes. "What are we doing, Logan?"

He smiled at her, but his eyes looked sad. "We're enjoying the time we've got. We're basking in the moment. Like it says to do in those self-help books you have scattered all over this house. Look, Allie, I'm not going to be here to help you for the next few months. But I want to do everything I can to help you now. I want to be here for you as much as I possibly can be, until I have to go."

And what about after that? The question jumped to her lips, but she pressed them tight and kept it inside. He wanted to be in the moment. What was so wrong with that? It was a pretty great moment. He was here. They were together. She was going to have a baby. And it was Christmastime.

Maybe she could be in the moment, too. Maybe everything else could wait.

"Okay," she said. "Okay."

And then the baby kicked hard, and he grinned, and looked down at her belly. "I think our child approves of your decision."

"*I* think we've got a black belt on our hands."

Logan let his hand trail over her abdomen and the baby kicked again. His eyes filled with wonder and joy. It was real. He wasn't faking that. She didn't really think he was faking anything.

Allie wondered how she was going to survive when he left her, and then she told herself there'd be enough time to miss him later. She didn't need to start right now.

"Adam's going to sleep at Angie's tonight," Logan whispered. "He's giving Jack his gift early. It's the newest Play Station. He says they're having a gaming marathon tonight."

"And…they didn't invite you?" she whispered.

"There are only two paddles," he said. "Thank goodness." He kissed her neck.

She shivered all over.

"Get down here, you two! Pizza's getting cold," Angie called.

So they did.

~

Everyone left. They were alone. They sat by the Christmas tree for a while, just basking in the twinkling lights. And then they went upstairs together, hand in hand, and he never took his eyes from hers as they undressed each other and fell into her bed together.

They kissed, and they touched. He made love to her without actually entering her—and she knew he was afraid he might hurt the baby. But it was beautiful, and it was blissful and fulfilling.

And falling asleep in his arms was absolute heaven.

CHAPTER TWELVE

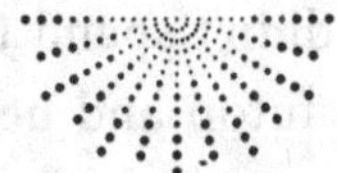

CHRISTMAS EVE

$\mathcal{A}$llie woke up warm and happy and more comfortable than she'd been in weeks. Logan was pressed up against her. One of his arms cradled her head and the other was wrapped around her waist. She felt perfect, and thought how good it would be to wake up like this every day. She wanted a life with him, and that terrified her, because she knew he was leaving and she was going to be broken-hearted.

She heard a knock at the front door and glanced at the clock. It was nine in the morning. She had no idea how she'd slept so late.

It took a lot of effort to extract herself from Logan's arms, and honestly, it wasn't something she wanted to do, but she finally managed to detangle herself without waking him up. She pulled on a snuggly robe and headed downstairs, opened the front door and greeted her sister who was smiling at her.

"What are you doing here?" Allie asked.

"Jack forgot a toy he can't live without." Angie came inside, shrugging out of her jacket and glancing around the place expectantly. The door to the den where Adam had been staying was open, his bed was still made up, nice and neat. She frowned and glanced toward the sofa, and then frowned even harder and looked up the stairs. "You um…you have any coffee, sis?" she asked.

"Not yet, but we can make some."

"Good." Angie headed for the kitchen and said, "I'm going to need a cup while you tell me why Logan is in your bed."

"What? What are you talking about, Logan's not—"

"Logan's not on the sofa. He's not in Adam's room—that is, the den. And I know he didn't spend the night in the nursery, because we took out the futon and he would never fit in that crib."

Allie opened her mouth, closed it again, and sank onto the stool at the kitchen island. She felt like she'd been keeping this secret forever. But she just didn't want to keep it any more. She wanted to tell Angie everything.

"I've seen the way he looks at you. Not to mention the way you look at him. There's something going on."

"Is it that obvious?"

"To me it is. To Mom, too. Dad and Adam are…well, they're guys." Angie took the carafe to the sink and filled it, then poured water into the coffee maker.

"It all started the night before Adam deployed," Allie began. And it was as if a dam inside her had broken, as her words and thoughts and feelings just spilled out of her.

By the time she had finished, the coffee was done, their mugs were half empty. The silence stretched and she looked at her sister, waiting for a reaction.

Angie was beaming. "This is wonderful!"

"What? No. This is a disaster. You heard the part where I said he's leaving, right?"

"Yeah. For three months. Three months is *nothing*. Hell, Jeff and I could do three months in our sleep. It'll be over before you know it. The point is, he's nuts about you, and I can tell from the look on your face that you're nuts about him, too."

"I…yeah. I am."

"Yeah, you are."

"But—"

"But nothing! Allie, this is a good thing. This is fate, practically hand-delivering your happily-ever-after to you. How could you even *think* about turning it down?

"I just…I don't think I can do it. I've been here. I've seen what you've gone through, losing Jeff. And the kids, what it's doing to them. I can't watch Logan leave and wonder if he's ever going to come home again. I can't let my baby go through that. I can't."

Angie's jaw tightened at the mention of Jeff's name and Allie could see the hurt in her eyes.

"Losing Jeff has been hard. But marrying him was the best decision I ever made. And yes, I'm hurting. There hasn't been a single day that I haven't thought about him, or wanted to share something with him and couldn't, or just plain ached for him. But you don't walk away from something good just because there's a chance you could lose it someday." Angie took a deep breath and sighed. "My heart breaks every day. But if someone gave me the chance to go back, I'd do it all over again. Knowing everything that was going to happen, I'd still do it all again. It's worth it, Allie. Jeff was worth it. What we had together was worth it. The years our kids had with the best dad on the planet were worth it. And I have a feeling that what you have with Logan is worth it, too."

Allie blinked back her tears.

"Allie, if you love him, then love him. Love him now, while he's here. Love him while he's away, and love him when he comes back. Love him as hard as you can for as long as you can. If you're lucky, that'll be a very long time. But I'm here to tell you honey, any time is better than none at all."

Angie's words stayed with Allie long after she'd left. They

ran through her mind all day, and every time she looked at Logan she heard them again.

~

The Long Branch Saloon had started a Christmas Eve tradition in Big Falls. They shut off the flow of alcohol for the evening, and Chef Ned prepared a feast fit for royalty. The whole town turned out, and everyone brought an ornament for the giant tree that filled the front windows of the dining room. Carols were sung, ornaments were hung, food was imbibed, and then they closed down early to get the little ones home in time for Santa.

White Christmas lights wound their way around curving bannisters to the second floor, where there were guest rooms. The place looked like a magical holiday wonderland.

Logan escorted Allie through the batwing doors. His black dinner jacket made his hair seem even darker and his blue eyes looked brighter in the glow of holiday lights. She'd heard that pregnancy made your hormones kick into overdrive, and she wondered if that was part of the reason she was so infatuated with Logan. But her heart knew better. Long after she had this baby, she was still going to be head over heels for this man. Her heart swelled.

She was in love with him.

"You look incredible," he whispered to her.

She didn't believe him for a second. She was wearing a red dress that fell just above the knee, but she knew at this point in her pregnancy everything looked basically the same. All her clothes became tent-shaped as soon as she put them on.

Throngs of people milled around the place. The owner, Joey McIntyre, was there with his wife Emily and their adorable little girl, Matilda. Allie's friend Kiley was there with her weeks-old baby girl and adoring husband Rob, and Kiley's sister Kendra, and most everyone else. Even Doc Sophie and her family were in attendance.

The red velvet curtains between the bar side of the place and the dining room side were held open with braided gold ropes. Some people stood, others sat at tables. And Santa—not Jack's Santa, she noted—was seated near the lighted tree, reading from a big hardcover edition of *The Night Before Christmas* to a group of awestruck children. This was the new addition to the Christmas Eve gathering that her father had been so excited about.

As he finished, Santa pulled out his pocket watch and looked at it as if surprised. "Oh my, it's getting late. I have some work to take care of tonight!" He waved to the children as he crossed the room, and they surrounded him all the way to the batwing doors. "Merry Christmas! Merry Christmas to all," he called. He went outside, and the kids raced back to the big windows to watch him go.

"Watch this," Allie whispered, pointing out the windows as Santa moved past them. He tapped the glass from outside and waved, and every child looked. Then he walked away, and a second later they heard the jingle of sleigh-bells and a projector flashed the image of a shadowy sleigh and reindeer across the cloudy sky. The children squealed with delight and laughter.

Logan smiled and squeezed her hand. "You were right about this town. It's magic. I'm so happy our baby is going to grow up here."

"Me, too."

Jack came running. The smile on his face was brighter than it had been in a year.

"Did you see that?" Jack asked

Allie hugged him. She hadn't mentioned their encounter with Santa Claus to her sister and now she was feeling guilty, wondering how the little boy would react when he woke up tomorrow morning. She leaned down until she was at eye level.

"Jack, I'm really glad you're so happy. I want you to have a great Christmas, and I don't want you to be disappointed if you don't get what you want."

Jack smiled. "Don't worry, Aunt Allie. I know it's not gonna happen this year. I might have to wait a long time, just like Logan did. But that *was* the real Santa. Daddy *is* gonna come home."

Allie would have argued, but her sister appeared then, and she didn't want to stress her out on Christmas Eve.

Angie gave her a hug. "Ready to go?" she asked Jack.

He nodded. "We have to get to bed early." Jack started off through the crowd and Angie hurried to catch up. "See you tomorrow," she called behind her.

Allie tried to focus on the festive party around her, but she was worried about her nephew.

"It's not your fault," Logan said as if reading her mind. "This was going to be tough for him no matter what you did. There's no way around that. At least this way he's not heartbroken."

Allie nodded. "Yeah, but he's not going to accept it, either."

Logan placed a finger under her chin and lifted it, so she looked up at him. "He wasn't accepting it any better before he talked to Santa, was he? Now how about I get you some punch? And it looks like they have cookies. Would you care to sample some?"

"That sounds nice."

Logan disappeared into the crowd and Allie found herself looking around the restaurant for familiar faces. She caught a glimpse of Adam standing just on the other side of the curtains, near the curving bar with its saddle shaped stools. He was speaking tersely to someone, and as Allie angled herself for a better view, she saw the woman shooting daggers back at him. Riley Everett, Adam's ex-wife, the PI who'd spent months trying to help Allie find Logan.

She squeezed her way through the crowd, her belly occasionally bumping into people as she passed. She was nervous and her stomach clenched, thinking about how angry her brother looked, and what he and Riley could possibly be talking about. Their marriage hadn't ended well.

She pushed her way through the crowd, but only in time to see them heading out through the batwing doors and into the cool Christmas Eve air of the parking lot outside. Of course she followed, this was her family.

"Why did you come back, Riley?" Adam demanded.

"I don't owe you any kind of explanation!"

"You never were big on explaining yourself, were you? You didn't even think you owed me an explanation when you walked out on our marriage."

"You not knowing why I left, that *was* the explanation." Riley tossed back the rest of her drink and stalked towards the entrance again.

Tough as nails Riley Everett had perfected her bitch face long ago, but her expression as she walked toward the restaurant was that of a woman who was barely holding it together. The anguish on her face only eased when she saw Allie standing there.

"Hey, Riley," Allie said.

Riley's eyes were filling with tears. She blinked them back, and wrapped Allie in a hug. "I shouldn't have come. I have some information for you, but this isn't the right time. I'm sorry." She kissed Allie's cheek.

Adam was right beside them now. "You did this?" he asked Allie. "You brought her here?" It was more an accusation than a question and it seemed to be exactly what Riley needed to pull herself together.

Her red curls bobbed as she spun around and leveled Adam with a cold glare. "I grew up here too, Adam. I have as much right to come home for Christmas as you do. And I divorced you. Not your family. If they need me, I'm going to be here."

"They don't need you. *We* don't need you."

"I needed her," Allie said, angry with her brother for treating Riley so badly. "I called her. She was helping me find the baby's father." She'd lied to Adam enough, so she figured giving him part of the truth was the best option.

Adam's angry expression rapidly turned shocked. "You told *her* who he is? You wouldn't even tell me. I could have helped. You didn't have to bring her into this." His voice was laced with pain and anger.

Allie felt responsible. Her head was throbbing and she felt her stomach clench. Stress. She was supposed to be avoiding it. "Please don't fight. This is my fault."

Allie heard the door and she turned around to see Logan, a worried look on his face.

Riley gaped. Then she looked at Allie again. "I guess you didn't need my help after all."

Logan looked confused and Allie felt like the world was dissolving around her. "What the hell is that supposed to mean?" Adam demanded. He aimed his angry look at Allie.

"Leave her alone." Logan's voice was deep and a little bit dangerous.

"Come on, Allie. Isn't it time we got everything out in the open?" Adam said.

Logan stepped in front of her. "Yeah, Adam. It's long past time."

Allie's head felt like it was going to explode, it was throbbing so hard. She closed her eyes just as a strong pain squeezed her abdomen.

"I'm the baby's father, Adam."

Adam's face turned from angry to completely blank. "That's… not possible. You met a week ago. How is that—"

Logan shook his head. "Allie was the girl I met before we deployed. I didn't know she was your sister until the airport."

Adam's hands fell to his sides. "You slept with my sister? And you stayed under the same roof as me this whole time and lied to me about it?"

He lunged at Logan a second before Allie squeezed her eyes shut. Logan pushed Allie backwards a step before the punch landed. She grabbed the split rail fence that bordered the parking lot, and then she forgot all about their stupid fighting, because her abdomen suddenly clenched so tight it felt as if she was a dish cloth being wrung out.

Adam socked Logan in the jaw, knocked him flat, then went down with him. Allie closed her eyes tight, but could still hear them scuffling around on the ground. Punches landed with ugly thuds. Riley cursed like a sailor at both of them.

When the pain let up enough that she could open her eyes, Allie saw that Logan's lip was bleeding and Adam's eye was bruising. She opened her mouth and yelled "Stop!"Riley grabbed Adam's shoulder and pulled him away from Logan. Adam shook off her hand.

Allie felt like a vice grip was being tightened around her abdomen. She gripped the railing waiting for it to end, but the pain only grew stronger. And then she heard Logan's voice. "Allie, are you all right?" He was at her side, one hand holding her elbow and the other around her waist.

She couldn't answer for a minute, but soon the pain started to ease and she could breathe again. She felt something warm trickling down her legs.

"No. I'm not all right. I'm in labor." She blinked a few times and looked at Logan. There was an expression of pure terror on his face.

"Someone call an ambulance!" Logan said.

Allie looked from Adam to Riley. Her ex-sister-in-law had gone white and she was pulling her cell phone out of her purse. She gave Allie a watery smile that didn't reach her eyes. "Don't panic. It's going to be okay." Her hand shook as she held the phone to her ear.

Another contraction tore through Allie's body, worse than the one before. "Logan, I'm scared," she whispered. "I think something's wrong."

~

The drive to the hospital in Tucker Lake dragged by. Logan raced behind the ambulance, where Doc Sophie, who'd been at The Long Branch, was riding with Allie. He was driving Allie's car and trying to figure out exactly what had gone wrong.

The doc wouldn't let him ride with Allie in the ambulance. She said she needed room to work, but every second apart from Allie brought another nightmare image. Something terrible could be happening to her, or the baby, or both of them, and his panic was so intense he wasn't sure he'd be able to breathe if he didn't see her soon.

Adam and Riley had climbed into the car with him. They were speaking low in the back seat. He wasn't listening. He couldn't care less what they had to say, the idiots, causing Allie all that stress when she was supposed to be avoiding it.

When he finally reached Tucker Lake General, he saw Doc Sophie and the EMTs, running through the ER doors with Allie on a stretcher.

He pulled to a stop beside a no parking sign, left the keys in the switch and jumped out of the car. Let Adam park the damn thing. Then he got out and ran through those doors, but didn't see her when he got inside.

The hospital was quiet. He didn't know where they had taken her or which way to go or who to ask for help. He stood there for a second, feeling helpless and scared. He hadn't felt that way since he was a kid, and he didn't like it.

He heard footsteps behind him and turned to see Adam and Riley running toward him. "Where is she?" Adam asked.

"I don't know," Logan said.

Riley rolled her eyes at both of them and hurried past them to the nurse's desk.

"We're looking for Alexis Wakeland. She just came in by ambulance."

"Are you family?" the nurse asked.

"I'm family, Adam said pushing his way toward the desk.

"We're *all* family," Riley said. "Can you tell us what's happening?"

She punched some keys on her computer and examined the screen. "She's not in the system yet. Wait right here. I'll see what I can find out."

Logan stared at the woman for all of thirty seconds before he gave up on that idea. He looked up and down the hall until he saw a map with arrows pointing to different areas. *Labor and Delivery, third floor.*

He took off in the direction of the elevator, refusing to wait another minute.

"Where the hell do you think you're going?" Adam asked, grabbing his arm.

"I'm going to find Allie. I need to know she's all right."

"You need to stay away from her. You need to get as far away from this hospital as you can before I lose the faltering hold I've got on my temper." Adam grabbed his arm, refusing to let him go any farther.

"Adam, I love you like a brother, but I'm going to find Allie, and I don't really care right now if I go with you or through you, I'm going."

"Then hurry the hell up," Riley said from behind them. "Adam, I swear to God, if you stop him from being with her right now, your sister will never forgive you. And neither will I." There was something in Riley's voice. Something that made it soft and shaky, but fierce.

Adam let go of Logan's shoulder all at once. He held his hand out to Riley for a brief second, but she shot a withering glare in his direction and he gave a nod. "Okay."

Logan hit the button for the elevator impatiently. "I'm sorry, Adam. I wanted to tell you the second I saw her, but I needed time to convince her we could do this."

"Do what, exactly? Just what the hell is going on between you and my sister? You barely know each other. What is this, a fling?"

"Not if I have anything to say about it." The elevator doors opened and all three of them crowded through. Logan jabbed the button for the third floor repeatedly until the doors slid closed.

"You love her?"

"Yeah," Logan said as the elevator climbed. "I do."

When the elevator doors slid open, Doc Sophie stood on the other side.

"I was just coming to find you. They've taken Allie to surgery."

"Surgery?" Logan thought he was going to vomit. "Surgery, why? What's wrong?

"They're doing a C-section. Look, it's gonna be okay. It's not as scary as it sounds."

Logan looked around helplessly. He didn't know what to do or how he could help. He just wanted to make it better. To fix whatever was wrong. Riley put a hand on his arm.

"She shouldn't be alone. Especially if…" Riley's voice trailed off. He didn't like that *if*. The way her voice wavered made his heart pick up speed. "You should be with her."

"Will they let me do that?" Logan asked.

"That's why I was coming to find you," Sophie said. "Follow me. We'll scrub in together." She turned and headed down the hall.

"Take care of her," Adam said.

Logan didn't have time to reply. He hurried after Doc Sophie, unable to speak or think or do much else except follow her down a hallway and into a room. "Wash your hands, arms to the elbows, and put on everything in that pile. *Over* your clothes. You wouldn't believe what happens when I forget to tell new fathers that."

That word nearly froze him in the spot. *Father.* He shook himself out of it long enough to follow her directions, donning a set of scrubs, a mask, a poufy hat, and shoe covers.

The doc did the same and then they were hurrying through another set of doors. Once he saw Allie, looking small and afraid in a sterile operating room, he forgot everything else. Tears were streaming down her face and before he even knew he had moved, he was standing next to her, holding her hand and wiping those tears from her eyes.

"I'm sorry, Allie. I'm so, so sorry. But I'm here now, and I'm not leaving you again." He said the words, even though he knew they weren't true. He knew he would have to leave and he knew it was gonna hurt like hell when he did.

She closed her eyes. She knew it, too.

"It's time to begin, folks," the doctor said. "I hope you've got a name picked out because you're about to be parents."

Allie squeezed his hand and Logan tried not to look at what the doctor was doing on the other side of the sterile barricade at Allie's middle. He could see everything reflected in the mirrored light over the bed and it was enough to scare the life out of him. He tried to stare at Allie's face instead. But soon he heard a soft strangled cry and he forgot that he was trying not to look. His eyes flew to the other side of the sheet and he caught sight of a beautiful pink-faced baby with a mass of black curls.

He wanted to jump and cheer and cry all at the same time. But then he felt Allie's hand slacken and fall out of his grasp. He tore his eyes away from their baby to look at her suddenly pale face. From the other side of the curtain he heard a flurry of activity and suddenly Doc Sophie was pulling him out of the room.

"I'm not leaving. I can't leave."

Logan felt helpless and terrified. Allie had become the most important thing in his world. He couldn't imagine a life without her.

Sophie gave him a firm shove. "The doctors need room to work. You can't help Allie right now, but your daughter needs you."

"My daughter?"

"Congratulations, Logan. It's a girl. You're a daddy."

Logan stood in a small, white room, pacing back and forth and waiting. He was trying to replay the events in his head. It didn't make sense to him. One minute Allie had seemed perfectly fine. She was upset, but she was okay. The next she had looked pale and weak and he couldn't get that image out of his mind. He didn't like picturing her like that. Didn't like seeing that image and imagining what might be going on now, but sitting in the empty hospital room, that was all he could do.

The door opened and he jumped up. Sophie wheeled a clear plastic bin into the room. It looked like something you would wash dishes in, but there, lying in the middle of the bassinet, was the most beautiful sight he'd ever seen. She was tiny and pink and fragile...with dark blue eyes in her elfin face.

"Have you heard anything?" He asked the question without taking his eyes off the baby. "How is Allie?"

"They just finished up. There was some unexpected bleeding. She lost a lot of blood. She's weak, but she's going to be all right."

A surge of relief washed over Logan. It was so strong he sank into the chair behind him unable to support the weight of it.

"I need to see her."

"It'll be a while."

Like hell, Logan thought.

"This isn't the time to be stubborn and pig headed." Doc Sophie seemed to be reading his thoughts. "She needs her rest. She's been through a lot. Besides, there's someone right here who needs some quality time with you." She picked up the newborn. "Do you want to hold her?"

"I…I've never held a baby this small before. Will I hurt her?"

"All new fathers ask that question. You'll be an expert in no time." She placed the baby in Logan's arms, showing him without words, how to cradle her properly.

He held her in his arms, his impossible small baby girl. He looked down at that face, and knew that nothing in his life was ever going to be the same again. Not ever.

He was in the same spot, still staring at that beautiful face ten minutes later when Adam entered the room.

"I'm not sure if you're ready for this," Adam said softly. "But we have a swarm of Wakelands in the waiting room waiting for a chance to meet the newest member of the family."

"Do they know…about Allie and me?"

"I gave them the condensed version."

"So, are you all gonna run me out of town on a rail?"

"That depends. Are you planning on sticking around to be part of this little girl's life?"

"For as long as your sister will have me."

"Then I think we'll be persuaded to take it easy on you. In the spirit of Christmas and all. Hell, even mean old Uncle Adam can't be mad when he's looking at that beautiful face."

"That's my girl," Logan said. "Not even a day old and she's already making miracles happen."

CHAPTER THIRTEEN

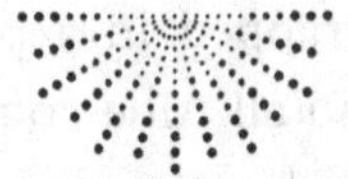

CHRISTMAS DAY

llie woke up feeling groggy and tired and sore. She felt worse than she'd ever felt in her life. Her mouth was dry, her head was pounding, and her entire body seemed to hurt. Her brain felt fuzzy and she couldn't seem to force her eyes to open.

Since her eyes refused to cooperate, she tried to focus on her other senses. She could smell antiseptic and she could hear voices. She focused on words, and waited for her body to catch up with her brain. Some of the fog began to clear and she was able to identify a voice. Logan's voice. The sound made her heart skip a beat. And then she remembered, and croaked, "My baby…"

She pried her eyes open and even the soft, dim light made them burn. She moaned.

"Allie?" He was beside her on the bed, perched on the edge and holding her hand. "There's so much I have to tell you, Allie."

She opened her eyes, staring as he slowly came into focus, and she wondered why she felt like crying. Their secret was out. Adam knew. Riley knew. Angie knew. And now it would just be a matter of time until Logan left and she was on her own.

He grabbed the pink plastic cup of ice water that was on the adjustable table by the bed and held it to her lips. She took a cool sip and felt the water soothe her parched throat.

Then Logan turned around and when he faced her again, he held their tiny baby in his arms. Their child.

"A girl," he said. "She's perfect and as beautiful as her mother."

Her daughter was wrapped in a pink blanket and wore a funny little striped hat, so all Allie could see was her pink face and one tiny fist that had escaped. Logan cradled her in his arms as if she was made of crystal, and his smile when he looked at the baby made her heart feel ten times its normal size. Tears welled in her eyes, tears of sheer joy.

He placed the baby in Allie's arms, settling himself beside her to help her hold on.

Love, that's what was filling her heart so much. More love than she'd ever felt before. More love than she even knew existed.

"We need a name for this little girl. I've been calling her peanut for the last few hours, but your mother didn't seem to approve of it as a long-term option."

"Mom's here?"

"Of course. The whole Wakeland Clan turned out."

"And…they know? About us?"

Logan smiled. "Oh yeah. I'm starting to think this was your plan all along. Wait until you're out of commission, so I have to confront an angry mob of Wakelands all on my own. It's a good thing I love you or I'm not sure I'd be so understanding."

Allie's head was swimming. Whether from the after effects of the anesthesia or his declaration of love, she couldn't be sure.

"You love me?"

He looked into her eyes then, and all the playful humor was gone. "I love you so much I can't stand it. You've gotta marry me, Allie. It'll kill me if you don't."

She gazed at their daughter and sniffled. "We barely know each other."

"I know your middle name is Mae and your favorite color is green. And you listen to every singer who's ever won *The Voice*. I know you start hanging Christmas lights the day after Halloween and that would drive me crazy if you were anyone else, but for you I'd climb on the roof in August and hang enough lights to make the house visible from space. I *do* know you. I might not know all there is to know about you yet, but I want to. I want to spend the rest of my life discovering everything about you, and making you happy. And raising our baby in your magical hometown. Together."

"But… but…" Tears were choking her, and she managed to tear her eyes from the baby and stare into his.

"But I have to leave. I know. It's going to be the hardest thing I've ever done, leaving you and our baby, but I'm coming back to you. For the first time, I have something to come back for. I have a home. A family. A crazy small town where everybody knows everybody else's business. A home. And I have you. I'll *always* come back to you. I love you."

Tears rolled down her cheeks. "I love you, too, Logan. I tried not to, but I love you to the moon and back."

Logan leaned down and kissed her, their baby daughter snuggled between them.

"Is that a yes?" he asked, his eyes so unsure, so afraid, that it touched her to her soul.

"Yes, Logan. Yes."

EPILOGUE

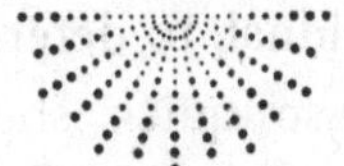

THREE MONTHS LATER

$\mathscr{A}$llie stood in the middle of a crowded military hangar trying to entertain a baby who'd been ready for a feeding and a nap an hour ago. Eliza Jane had changed a lot in the last three months. She was no longer tiny and fragile. Her face had grown round and her arms and legs were plump instead of scrawny. Allie was still sure there was nothing more precious in all the world.

She bounced with the baby in her arms. Allie had grown so accustomed to bouncing little Eliza that she found herself bopping up and down even when she wasn't holding the little girl. She blamed lack of sleep and an abundance of maternal instinct.

"How much longer?" Allie asked.

Her sister Angie stood by her side. "I've been to tons of military homecoming ceremonies, and the only thing that's certain is that they're never the same. Sometimes they keep you waiting for hours and sometimes they're right on schedule, but no matter what, it always feels like an eternity."

"Are you sure you're okay with this?" Allie asked. "Is it too much for you?"

Angie smiled and grabbed the camera that hung around her neck. "There's no place I'd rather be."

The wide-open hanger was decorated with balloons and streamers and signs welcoming family members home. There were people everywhere, but Allie ignored all of it because at that moment, the big double doors opened and soldiers began marching through them. Allie's breath caught in her throat. She tried to study each individual, to determine which one was *her* soldier, but they came so quick she barely had time. She scanned the sea of faces, standing in smart-lines, wearing their dress uniforms. She was looking for Logan as the commander talked with pride about the job his soldiers had done.

She tried to focus on the words, but she was too excited to think. The butterflies in her stomach felt like bats. After three long months of waiting, and talking and texting and Facetiming, she was about to see her husband again, and her heart practically sang. Eliza must have known it, too, because she perked up in Allie's arms, looking around excitedly, taking in the lights and the people. She let out an ear-splitting yell that broke the relative quiet.

The commander smiled. "Someone's impatient," he said and just like that, he gave the order, and the soldiers were released. Then it was a sea of loved ones making their way to each other, of hugs and kisses and whoops of joy and men picking up women and spinning them in circles.

Allie scanned the crowd around her, searching for Logan. She turned around, desperate to see the face she'd been dreaming of for the last ninety days. And then there he was, right in front of her. Logan. She ran to him and he wrapped his arms around her and their precious baby. Tears filled her eyes. Logan's lips found hers and he kissed her. And everything around them vanished, the noise, the crowds. There was nothing but the three of them.

He gazed at the baby in Allie's arms. Eliza smiled and let out a happy squeal and Logan laughed. Tears filled his eyes.

"I'm home," he said.

"Not yet, honey. Home is in Big Falls. We've got a drive ahead of us."

"Home is wherever you are, Allie. It's wherever both of you are."

"It's wherever the three of us are, together," Allie told him. And then she kissed him again.

THE END

**Continue reading for an excerpt from Book 6 in the
McIntyre Men Series
Oklahoma Sunshine**

PREVIEW OKLAHOMA SUNSHINE

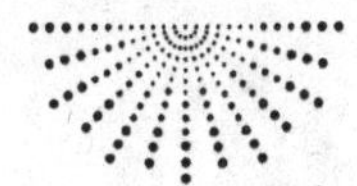

CHAPTER ONE

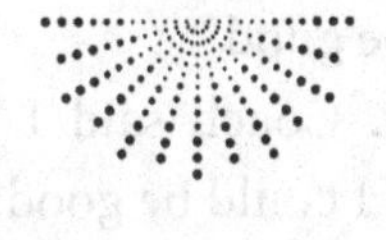

15 YEARS AGO

Mary braced up when she approached her dad. She was as likely to get backhanded as not, so she always braced up when she left her room in whatever house they lived in. Right now it was a doublewide with three whole bedrooms in the woods outside town. Three bedrooms meant she got one of her own. If there were only two, she'd have to sleep on the couch, and she hated sleeping on the couch because it smelled like beer and cigarettes.

Her dad was sitting at the kitchen table. He was drinking a beer, smoking a cigarette, and eating a peanut butter chocolate chip cookie. She'd baked a big batch yesterday, and it had put him in a good mood for all of ten minutes.

Her mom used to bake. She didn't remember, but he'd said so often enough.

That he was eating the cookie was a good sign, but that he was looking at the 'net cancelled it out. The internet always got him going. Maybe this wasn't the best time. Her brother Braxton was with him. Brax was eight and already hated her guts. And he was *always* with their father. She stood still a minute trying to decide.

"Spit, it out kid. What do you want now?" her father asked without looking up from his computer.

She took a deep breath, lifted her chin. "I want to play softball."

"*Soft*ball? Psssh. Softball. You getting this Brax? Little Mary Sunlight wants to play softball. What makes you think you'd even make the cut, kid? They have tryouts for that sort of thing, you know. You have to be good."

"Tryouts were today. Coach said I have the makings of a great pitcher. She thinks I could be good."

Her brother made big eyes at her. "*You* made the team?"

"Only two other fifth graders got picked. Everyone else is older."

"I bet the competition was *fierce*," her father said, making it clear he meant the opposite. "Softball. Jeeze, if you play anything, you oughtta pick a real sport."

She did not back down. It was really hard to disagree with her father, and she knew was risking a solid backhand across the face by trying. But this was important to her. "I'll have to stay after school for practice during the season, but there's a late bus so you won't have to pick me up or anything."

"And who the hell's gonna make dinner if you're off playing softball? You ungrateful little shit."

She closed her eyes, cowed and frightened. But this was important. Head low, voice soft, she said, "I'll still have dinner on the table by six, Dad. And on game nights, I'll cook ahead of time so all you'll have to do is heat it up."

"She sure as hell won't have time for desserts," Braxton complained, not to her, to their old man. He barely bothered to acknowledge her as a living being. She was more like a piece of furniture to him.

"I'll do all the baking for the week on weekends," she said. "That's not hard. Anyway, it would save on the gas bill, baking everything at once."

He father narrowed his eyes and looked right at her, instead of through her. "I don't like it. Girls aren't meant to play sports. It'll turn you."

Her brother laughed, and started singing, "Mary's a lesbo, Mary's a lesbo..."

Her cheeks burned. "If I don't play, people are gonna wonder why. Everyone at school saw the tryouts." There was nothing her father hated more than school officials poking around his life. He'd given her a black eye once, and her teacher had asked her over and over what happened. She might've given different answers on different days, though she'd never ratted out her father. Still, social services had shown up at the front door a few days later.

He had never hit her where it would show again. So, she knew he feared that, if he feared anything.

He thought for a long time, then took another bite of the cookie. "The first time you're late or I go hungry, it ends." Then, just to show he wasn't really giving in, he elbowed Brax. "I give it a week, how 'bout you?"

"Three days. She's lazy, and the softball players have to run laps."

They laughed together. Mary turned and went back to her room.

"Aw, I think you hurt her feelings. Your feelings hurt, Little Mary Sunlight? Are they?"

She closed her bedroom door, careful not to slam it. If she slammed it, he'd surge in there like a bull and knock her around to teach her some respect. She hated when he called her Mary Sunlight. Her mother used to call her that. Sometimes, she'd just hold her close and dance around the room, singing "Little Mary Sunlight" to her. It was one of a handful of foggy memories that were all she had of her mom. Becky Beauregard had died a long, long time ago.

Mary took the framed photograph off its crooked nail in the

wall and traced her mother's face. She was so beautiful, hair just like sunshine, and that sunny smile on her face, too. She wore a pretty dress, pale blue, and white beads around her neck, pearls or whatever.

"Why'd you have to die?" she whispered. Tears welled up and rolled down her cheeks.

CHAPTER TWO

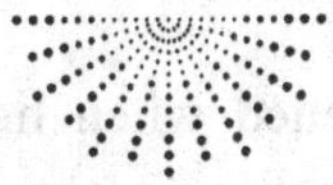

PRESENT DAY

Jason swung the hammer in a steady, soothing cadence. Around and down. Around and down. Every blow shaped the red-hot steel on the anvil more. His body was damp with sweat, both from the heat of the forge and the exertion of swinging that hammer.

The trick was to get in as many blows as possible before the metal began to cool. And there was a knack to knowing just when that was. One swing too many, the blade cracks, and it's over.

But it wouldn't take too many more. This beauty was nearly done. He took the smaller hammer and went up and down the blade, perfecting the shape. And then he heated it once more, gave a final inspection, and doused it in a vat of oil.

The hiss of the steam from the oil and the smell of hot metal were satisfying in a way he could never describe to anyone else, which was why he hadn't bothered to try.

This was *his* thing. He didn't share it.

Using the tongs, he took the blade out, held it at arm's length, tipped it left and right as he eyed its edge. Not a ripple. Not a bend. Perfection. It was ready to be honed, polished. He had a handle ready and waiting; intricately carved bone in the shape of an elk's head, stylized, long and slender, but you could still tell what it was.

He put the blade on the workbench, took off his goggles, his apron, his oversized leather gloves, and shut down the forge. And only when everything in the workshop was where it belonged, did he go back inside and straight through to the shower.

And as always happened when he wasn't working at the forge, his brain kicked into overdrive. He'd been working day and night to avoid thinking about what needed thinking about, but he had to stop sometime. He had to think sometime. He couldn't put this off much longer.

He was going to propose to Sunny Cantrell, the sweetest girl in Oklahoma.

He cranked the knobs, stripped down and stepped into the spray. Then he washed and worried until a voice coming from his living room forced him to call it. Grabbing a towel and wrapping it around him, he opened the door a crack to peer out. His brother Rob stood there grinning at him. Jason gave a quick look at his shop door to be sure it was closed. It was.

"I brought you a beer," Rob said, holding up the bottle.

"That's perfect. I was just wishing for a beer. Gimme a sec?"

Rob nodded, sashaying into the living room to plunk himself on the sofa and twist the cap off his long neck. Wrapped in a towel, Tarzan style, Jason left wet footprints all the way to his bedroom where he pulled on a pair of pants. He scrubbed his hair with the towel on his way back out, tossed it behind him and missed the hamper.

"What brings you here, little bro?"

"My better half, mainly."

Jason went to the easy chair, picking up his beer on the way by. "Kiley sent you?"

"Yeah, with a message."

"For me? You sure it's not for Sunny?" Sunny and Kiley and Angie Wakeland had been hanging out since last summer. All the girls were friendly, but that trio had become really tight.

"No, it's for you. It's *about* Sunny, though."

"Well, by all means, deliver the message." He tipped his bottle Rob's way.

Rob stood up and cleared his throat. "Sunny Cantrell is the prettiest, happiest, most successful female in this town, and I have lost my baby weight now—"

"You have, have you?"

Jason scowled at him. "This is Kiley talking."

"I don't think so. Her voice is higher, and she's easier on the eyes."

"Do you mind if I finish?"

He waved a hand. "I can hardly wait."

"I have lost my baby weight now and will look great in my bridesmaid's gown. So get your ass in gear before some other guy comes along and steals her right out from under your slow-moving nose."

He just sat there a sec. Rob returned to his seat, took his beer off the coffee table and drank a big gulp.

"That's quite the message."

"Yeah." He burped. "The beer was my idea. You're welcome."

"Huh. I gotta say, her timing is interesting. Stay right there." He got up, went into the kitchen, opened a cabinet and took out a box of brownie mix.

"Are we baking, bro?"

"Nah. It's the only place I knew she'd never find it. She wouldn't be caught within ten feet of a mix." He opened the box, tipped it up, and out came the little white box.

Rob jumped to his feet. "Holy Smokes, you're really gonna do it!" He surged to the kitchen and snatched the ring box right out of his hand.

"I really am."

Rob opened the box and turned it one way and another to make the diamonds sparkle. "I think Kiley will approve."

Jason took the box back, snapped the lid closed. "Yeah, well, don't tell her. No point in her being disappointed if Sunny says no."

"What the—Sunny isn't gonna say no. Why would she say no? You two have been seeing each other for what, four years now?"

"Almost five." He put the ring back in the brownie box, returned it to the cupboard, top shelf, way back.

"She actually might. I would've popped the question before now, otherwise, but every time I bring up anything about…you know, a future together, she gets all funny."

"Funny how?" Rob asked.

"Funny like she suddenly has to leave, or go to the bathroom, or she spills her sweet tea or something."

"On purpose?"

Jason shrugged.

"So, if you don't think she wants it, then why are you asking?"

He heaved a huge sigh. "Because *I* want it. And if she doesn't, well at least she'll have to say so."

Rob whistled a pretty good impression of a bomb falling as he dropped onto the sofa and said, "I think we're gonna need more beer."

"I just…this feels so stupid. What are we, teenage girls?"

"Yeah, we're teenage girls. Tell me what's going on with you, Jason. I'm your brother, come on."

Jason took a deep breath. "I want what you and Joey have. And I want kids. Every time I hold your little Diana or take Matilda Louise on a piggy back ride, I just about lose it. I want a family and I want it with her."

"And you don't think she wants that, too?"

"That's what I'm about to find out." He went back to the kitchen, picking up his brother's empty on the way.

"When? Today?"

"Tonight, I hope."

"And I can't tell Kiley?"

"No, because she'll tell Sunny—instantly. And you know it."

"Yeah," he said. "I know it. But damn, when I get home, she's gonna want to hear how this all went. You know, what you said when I gave you the message."

"Tell her I said thanks for caring, and I'm taking it under advisement."

~

The text that popped up on Sunny's cell phone said, "We need to talk. Can I come over tonight?"

Sunny was at the bakery's front counter counting up the day's take and putting the cash into a bank bag. She set the bag down and stared at the phone. Her heart sank a little.

"Everything okay, boss?

She glanced up at Mouse, who'd got his nickname as much for his large ears as for his actual first name, Mickey. He'd just finished mopping the main floor and was pushing his wheeled bucket toward the back. "Everything's fine, Mouse. You go on home, you're done for the day."

"On my way."

"Oh, and take this box of pastries with you for Ida Mae." She set the box up on top of the counter, which was really a chest-high glass display case with shelves inside, and a cash register on top.

"Mmm, cheese danish?"

"Go ahead and snatch one for yourself before you hand 'em over. These are leftovers."

He looked up, one brow bent. "But you always send the leftovers to the Tucker Lake Shelter."

Mickey was a former resident of the Tucker Lake Shelter.

That was where she'd met him, back when she used to drive the extra baked goods over there herself. "There's plenty for the shelter, I promise. I saved a dozen extra for Ida Mae, and one for you. Go on."

He looked at the box and smiled. "Miss Ida Mae will offer me first choice from the box when I hand it to her. I think she's nursing a crush on me."

He was forty-something. Ida Mae was seventy-something. But she loved having Mickey there. He mowed her lawns, tended her flowers and did light repairs in exchange for room and board. He'd fixed up the second story of the old detached carriage house, and worked at the bakery for pocket-money. He was as happy as a millionaire.

He gave her a nod and a smile, took the box, and headed back.

"Tell Tabitha she can go, too, if she's still in the kitchen."

"Don't worry about that one. Tabitha leaves at five. Not one minute later."

"Gotta love a girl who knows her worth smack outta high school. G'night, Mouse."

"Night, Miss Sunny."

He pushed the mop bucket through the double doors into the kitchen.

Sunny picked up her phone again, re-read the message, and knew what it meant. Jason was going to break up with her. She'd been expecting it for a while now, and while she hated that it was going to happen, she knew it had to. Jason wanted more, she knew he did. He'd brought it up enough times. But she couldn't. She just couldn't.

She'd tried hard not to let things get too serious between them. But as much as she'd held back, she'd become powerfully attached to him. And she cared about him. And she loved being with him. When he wasn't hinting about their future.

They didn't *have* a future.

She should've told him that from the beginning, but she hadn't, and before she knew it, she'd waited too long. So they'd been doing this dance for five years now—dating, hanging out together, sleeping together, attending all his huge family's events together. And all the while, with him trying to get closer and her trying not to.

He wanted more. He was the most eligible bachelor in the state of Oklahoma. He deserved to have what he wanted.

She looked down at the phone. His text looked back at her, unanswered. *We need to talk.* This was kind of heartbreaking. The two of them were good together. She liked having someone who was kind of hers. And he was a good man. A great man, really.

Best man she'd ever known.

She picked up the phone and typed "Just closing up," sent it and realized she was still avoiding the inevitable. Time to face the music. She couldn't get serious with him, and she couldn't tell him why not, and he deserved more. So she keyed in more. "Meet you in the pavilion down back?" It was, she figured, as good a place to be dumped as any, and a better place than most. It was her favorite spot. She almost decided to take it back, suggest somewhere else instead, but he was already replying. The ellipsis dots blinked a coming attraction.

The bell over the door jangled, but she didn't look up until the text came through. "I'll be there in an hour."

"Ah, hell," she whispered.

"Bad news?" Jack Kellogg, her best friend Kiley's father, came up to the counter, smiling his charming smile, dimples digging deep into his cheeks.

"Of course not." She put the phone down and greeted him with her usual sunny smile.

"I've always wondered if that's short for anything. Sunny."

"Nope." She set the phone down. "What can I do for you, Jack?" She wasn't fond of Jack Kellogg. He reminded her of people and things she'd rather forget. He'd done time. But he was Kiley's father, and had allegedly reformed his con-man ways. Because of that, she tried to be polite to Jack and Kendra, Kiley's twin sister, another reformed criminal. But as far as she was concerned, the two of them were not to be trusted.

"Looks like you're closing up. I don't want to–"

"I got distracted and didn't turn the sign over, but don't give it another thought."

"I promised Diana a cookie," he said. "And if I don't bring one back, I'll lose grandpa points."

Kiley and Rob's little girl. Sunny's heart melted at the mention of her name. Both her best friends had children, and she soaked up every bit of kid-time she could, knowing she'd probably never have a family of her own.

"Halfmoons are her favorite," Sunny said. "Wait here." She started to go, then remembered the bank bag was still sitting on the counter. But there was just no discreet way to pick it up now without being obvious. And she didn't want to hurt his feelings.

She sent Jack a smile and headed back into the kitchen, where the leftovers from the day were ready for delivery to the Tucker Lake Shelter. She put four halfmoon cookies into a pink box with white stripes. Her boxes were just like her awning. Each one bore the logo that was also painted on her front window, a bright yellow sun, with SUNNY'S PLACE spelled out above and below, each letter set within a curvy golden ray.

She didn't go behind the counter, and she made herself *not* look at the bank bag as she met Jack in front of it. "Here you go. One for everybody."

"Including me?"

"Including you."

He smiled and said, "You can check if you want. Your money bag's still there."

"Wh-what do you mean?"

"You went back and left an ex-con with your lettuce, so you wouldn't hurt his feelings. You risked a sack of cash just to be nice. Maybe even trusted me a little. I can't even get that much out of my daughter." He gave a shrug and a smile. "Yet."

He handed her a ten-dollar bill, she waved him off. "I already tallied up for the day. These cookies have been written off. If I charge you, I'll go to tax jail."

He took a deep breath, like he was going to say something, but then lowered his head and turned to go.

"What? What were you going to say?"

He looked over his shoulder. "I uh...I have a past. You know that."

"Everyone knows that. It's a small town." But no one knew about hers. She was living a lie in plain sight, and sooner or later, it was bound to come out. She dreaded that day. Jason flashed in her mind's eye, and her heart broke a little. She'd been fighting not to fall in love with him for years.

Jack turned around to face her again, like he'd changed his mind about leaving. "I uh—I don't like when people from my past start coming around Big Falls. I'm a grandpa now. A very young, very handsome grandpa."

"Modest, too," she said smiling. But it felt odd, this conversation. They knew each other, were even friendly, but they didn't talk. Not like this.

"Is someone from your past in town, Jack?"

"Someone I knew in passing yeah. Not to see me—I doubt he even knows I'm here. But you know, I keep up with a few old friends, so I hear things. He's bad news, this guy."

She wanted to ask why he was telling her this, but thought it would be rude. He seemed to really want to get it out. He wouldn't be the first local to come to her out of the blue, wanting to talk out a problem. People really seemed to think she had it all figured out, didn't they? God, if they only knew.

He was quiet. Expectant, so she said, "Do you have any idea what he wants in Big Falls?"

"Maybe." He shrugged and looked at his toes. "It's not good, whatever it is."

"Why don't you tell Chief Jimmy?"

"Yeah, I'm still not real comfortable around the law."

"He's not the law, Jack. He's family."

"I think you're stretching it there. He's my son in law's step-brother-in-law. We live up to the stereotype, don't we?"

"I'm not related, and they all feel like family to me. I love that about this town."

"You *are* family to Kiley. And little Diana lights up every time she sees you. I've got a lot to make up for with my girls. So, I wanted to give you a heads-up."

She was still puzzled, but she thought she saw something in Jack she hadn't before. Maybe he really was trying to be a better person. Maybe they weren't so different, the two of them.

And then he brought his head up real slow, looked right into her eyes. "This guy who's on his way here, his name's Braxton Hayes."

Everything in her—body, blood, breath, bone—spun into a whirlpool that had opened under her feet. She was clawing to hold onto the edges, to keep from falling into the dark vortex. And she did it. She held on, palms flat to the counter. No more than a second had passed. Jack might've noticed. He might not. Hell, he might already know.

It had been a long, long time since she'd heard her brother's name. And Jack Kellogg, alleged master of the con, not long out of prison, felt compelled to walk in here and tell her that Brax was coming for her just like she'd always known he would.

"Thanks for the cookies," Jack said, all easy and smooth, like he didn't know that he'd just set her world on fire. Trying to read his face was a waste of time. It only showed what he wanted her to see. Schoolboy dimples and mischievous Newman-blue eyes. "So long, Sunny. You take care, now."

He was out the door before she'd regained the power of speech. She closed her eyes. Opened them again. She wanted to believe it was coincidence, that Jack had just come in here and spilled his guts to her like a drinker to a bartender. Instead of alcohol, she served sugar. And weren't they sort of the same thing?

But no. It had been no accident. Jack had walked in to warn her, and that meant he knew.

And if he knew, her life in Big Falls was over.

"Oh, no," she whispered. "Oh no."

ALSO AVAILABLE

The McIntyre Men
Oklahoma Christmas Blues
Oklahoma Moonshine
Oklahoma Starshine
Shine On Oklahoma
Baby By Christmas
Oklahoma Sunshine

The Oklahoma Brands
The Brands who Came for Christmas
Brand-New Heartache
Secrets and Lies
A Mommy For Christmas
One Magic Summer
Sweet Vidalia Brand

ABOUT THE AUTHOR

New York Times and *USA Today* bestselling novelist Maggie Shayne has published sixty-two novels and twenty-two novellas for five major publishers over the course of twenty-two years. She also spent a year writing for American daytime TV dramas *The Guiding Light* and *As the World Turns*, and was offered the position of co-head writer of the former; a million-dollar offer she tearfully turned down. It was scary, turning down an offer that big. But her heart was in her books, and she'd found it impossible to do both.

In March 2014, she did something even scarier. She left the world's largest publisher and went "indie."

Now, she is embarking on an exciting new leg of her publishing journey, with most of her titles moving to small press publisher, Oliver Heber Books.

Maggie writes small town contemporary romances like the recent *Bliss in Big Falls* series, which boasts "a miracle in every story."

She cut her teeth on western themed category romances like her classic 90s and early 2000s *The Texas Brand* and *The Oklahoma All-Girl Brands,* and later expanded into romantic suspense and thrillers like *The Secrets of Shadow Falls* and *The Brown and de Luca Novels.*

She is perhaps best known for her beloved paranormal romances, like the brand new *Fatal series* and perennial favorites *The Immortals,* the *By Magic series,* and *Wings in the Night.*

Maggie is a fifteen-time RITA® Award nominee and one-time winner. She lives in the rolling green and forested hilltops of Cortland County NY, wine & dairy country, despite having sworn off both. She is a vegan Wiccan hippy living her best life with her beloved husband Lance, and usually at least two dogs.

Maggie also writes spiritual self-help and runs an online magic shop, BlissBlog.org

Visit Maggie at www.maggieshayne.com